Jake suddenly kn...
was the first.

Her first? Was it possib...

He used the last bit of ... his elbows and look do... ... her. Her face was the picture of abandon, her hair a wild carpet spread out across the pillows.

This was too big a gift for him to take without words. "Mary."

She'd closed her eyes and arched her neck. He tried not to look.

"Mary, listen to me." Desperation colored his efforts. Jake fisted his hands in her hair and forced her attention. "Are you sure? Sure it's me you want? You don't even know me."

She stared up at him with heavy-lidded eyes, her lips slightly parted and her chest heaving. His mouth went dry as she bit on her bottom lip and tried to smile.

"I chose you because you're a good person. A kind and careful soul who cares about being somebody's first."

Jake started to shake his head, to deny what she'd said. He was far removed from anyone who resembled such a description. But she didn't know it. Couldn't know it.

Become a fan of Silhouette Romantic Suspense books on Facebook and check us out at www.eHarlequin.com!

Dear Reader,

Once again Silhouette Romantic Suspense authors are happy to bring you a compelling story from the Colton family. This branch of the Coltons is headquartered in Montana, and we had lots of fun developing the intrigue between three powerful families living in the small town of Honey Creek.

Covert Agent's Virgin Affair is book #2 in the six-book series and I really enjoyed writing it. Both my hero and heroine had damaging pasts and I wasn't sure they could ever overcome them in order to find happiness together. But I love my heroine, who has just lost over a hundred pounds and is ready to start a new life. Mary's a special person who deserves a special love, and I think she finds it in the man who is ready to die to save her life. But the trick for Mary is to open her eyes and see who the man she loves really is underneath his shell.

Thanks for coming along on the journey. Hope you enjoy reading the Coltons' stories as much as we enjoyed writing them!

Happy reading!

Linda Conrad

LINDA CONRAD

Covert Agent's Virgin Affair

ROMANTIC
SUSPENSE

Special thanks and acknowledgment to
Linda Conrad for her contribution to
THE COLTONS OF MONTANA miniseries.

 SILHOUETTE BOOKS

Recycling programs
for this product may
not exist in your area.

ISBN-13: 978-0-373-27690-5

COVERT AGENT'S VIRGIN AFFAIR

Books by Linda Conrad

LINDA CONRAD

When asked about her favorite things, Linda Conrad lists a longtime love affair with her husband, her sweetheart of a dog named KiKi and a sunny afternoon with nothing to do but read a good book. Inspired by generations of storytellers in her family and pleased to have many happy readers' comments, Linda continues creating her own sensuous and suspenseful stories about compelling characters finding love.

A bestselling author of more than twenty-five books, Linda has received numerous industry awards, among them the National Readers' Choice Award, the Maggie, the Write Touch Readers' Award and the *RT Book Reviews* Reviewers' Choice Award. To contact Linda, read more about her books or to sign up for her newsletter and/or contests, go to her Web site at www.LindaConrad.com.

To Marie, Jennifer, Cindy, Beth and Karen.

What a pleasure it was to work with you!
Let's do it again!

And to Patience Smith, who came up with
the spark that started it all. You continue to be the
editor extraordinaire!

My many thanks to all of you for making this a great
book and a fun time!

Chapter 1

As the first blow crashed into his right shoulder, FBI special agent Jake Pierson wasn't thinking about self-defense. He'd been deep in his head, preparing and memorizing backstory for his latest undercover assignment.

Standing alone in the delivery zone behind a hotel bar after sundown without backup wasn't the smartest move for a special agent, even one undercover. But Jake was waiting for the contact to let him know when his target had entered the bar.

He'd done his pre-mission checking and considered the medium-size western city of Bozeman, Montana, a safe place after dark. Apparently, he was wrong.

But it didn't take him ten seconds to get back in the game. Jake's body curved backward as the assailant pressed a thumb to his windpipe. If it hadn't been such a surprise, Jake might've laughed at the amateurish attempt at overpowering someone like him, well-trained in martial arts. But the sudden knee to his kidney switched the mood from light to serious in a flash.

Planting his feet, Jake bent at the knees and burst upright with a roar. Power-lifting had been one of his specialties during training at Quantico, and he hadn't tried a move like this in the many years since.

The assailant clung to his neck. Jake easily rolled him over his shoulder and slammed him to the ground.

In seconds the attacker jumped back to his feet. Jake had to hand it to him, the guy was resilient.

Suddenly a knife appeared, and the man was waving it in Jake's face. In the low light it was hard to tell, but Jake figured this was a kid. At least ten to fifteen years younger than his own ancient age of thirty-five.

What was this? A robbery attempt? Or something more?

Jake would have to ask the asshole. As soon as he disarmed him.

The kid's knife hand swung wildly, and when Jake sidestepped, the assailant threw himself off balance. Jake used the opportunity to grab him by the elbow and twist the attacker's whole arm up and behind his back.

"Ow!" The kid screamed like a child on a Ferris wheel and dropped his knife.

Jake whirled him around and slammed the heel of his hand square in the assailant's nose. The blow reverberated back up Jake's arm, but the sickening sound of breaking cartilage told him his attacker would be hurting a lot worse than he was.

"My nose. You broke my frigging nose!" The kid started throwing punches without looking.

Jake sighed, wishing the kid would simply go down easy. He hated having to inflict more damage in order to subdue an obvious nonprofessional.

"Hey, what's going on out here?"

A sudden bright light from the bar's open back door, along with the sound of someone shouting, took Jake's attention away from his assailant. For only an instant. But it was enough time for the kid to get in one last smash at Jake's side and then break away. Jake stumbled to the left while the kid made a mad dash down the side of the building and out of sight.

It took everything Jake had in him not to chase after his attacker. *The mission always comes first.*

The bartender stepped beside Jake. "Are you okay? You want me to call the cops?"

Jake straightened up as he shot the wrinkles out of his lightweight leather jacket. "No need to call anyone. It was a simple misunderstanding."

The last thing he needed was for the Bozeman cops to question him. If this attack had come twenty miles south in the little town of Honey Creek where Jake's main assignment would be taking place, talking to the sheriff wouldn't be a problem. The sheriff there knew the FBI would be in his town conducting an undercover operation. But here? Not worth all the effort.

"Well, if you're sure." The bartender shrugged. "Oh, yeah. The reason I stepped out here is that woman you were asking about is in the bar. She came in with several friends, but they're gone now. She's sitting at a small table all alone. Is that what you wanted?"

"Good work." Jake shoved a few bills into the

bartender's hand. "Remember not to tell anyone I was asking. Right?"

"Yes, sir." The bartender grinned and put his fingertip to his lips.

Annoyed that he hadn't been able to question his attacker, Jake tried to tell himself that it must have been a simple robbery attempt. But his gut told him that wasn't true. It would've been a huge coincidence, and Jake had never believed in coincidences.

Foul-ups on this job had started from the get-go. The man he was supposed to meet in Honey Creek had turned up dead a few days ago—before he could tell Jake anything. That put a giant kink in the FBI's information stream.

Jake had frantically put together a fall-back plan with the help of Jim Willis, his partner back in Seattle. He'd spent most of the past twenty-four hours memorizing facts and backgrounds that Jim had supplied.

Following the bartender inside, Jake rubbed at the knuckles on his right hand, absently opening and closing the fingers. He stopped to stand in the shadows behind the bar, taking time to study his new target and running over what he knew of her in his head.

Late twenties with shoulder-length bright red hair, she was one of his original informant's two daughters. The other daughter reportedly kept nearly constant company with a new boyfriend, whereas this one, a single, quiet librarian, seemed like a much easier mark. In addition, the *other* daughter also had more involvement in the secondary aspects of this case. For one thing, she'd had at least one good reason to want to see her father dead.

When Jake finally spotted his target in a far corner,

the sudden kick of attention from his libido surprised the hell out of him. Where had that come from? He hadn't taken much interest in the opposite sex beyond a few brief liaisons in the past ten years. And it would not have been his choice to start noticing again in the middle of an undercover mission. The timing was inopportune at the very least.

Then again… He reconsidered the idea as he continued studying the woman who was sipping wine and flirting casually with the bartender. Maybe his own…uh…interest would add a layer of reality to the mission. He and his partner Jim had devised a plan calling for Jake to pretend a romantic relationship with this target. The idea was to insinuate himself with her first. Then she would introduce him to the rest of her family and the others in Honey Creek while he took his time gathering information.

Jake suddenly thought *pretending* a romantic relationship might not be such a hardship. *The mission always comes first.*

Mary Walsh fidgeted in her seat and sneaked a glance around the bar. Maybe she was being foolish. Coming to a librarians' conference and expecting to find a wonderful stranger who would introduce her to the joys of womanhood seemed a bit incongruent. Probably there wouldn't be one real man in this whole hotel.

But Mary was determined to find out in the little time she had left at the conference. Her life was already changing, enough, in fact, that she could scarcely keep up. For one thing, her father, the one who had supposedly died fifteen years ago, had suddenly turned up dead—again! She had barely managed to put all her baggage behind her and now she was facing memories of her childhood one more time. Damn him anyway.

Mary took a sip of her wine and tried to calm down. Then, staring absently at the remaining rose-colored liquid, she winced. Her therapist would have his own breakdown if he knew she was using alcohol as a substitute for food. He expected her to go for a nice long run instead.

But, well, screw him. *He* wasn't the one who'd had to fight hard to change his whole life. And after coming this close to her ultimate goal, *she* was the one who'd been smacked in the face with the same old problems she'd thought were far behind her, not her therapist.

After all, who else in the entire world but the Walsh family would have a father who'd died not once but twice, for pity's sake?

She raised her hand and signaled to the bartender for another wine. A new start. That was what she needed. She was all done preparing for life. This latest mess her father had brought down upon the family had clinched it for her.

Mary was ready to start living.

"Hey. This seat taken?" The deep male voice brought her head up and she stared into the most wonderful pair of ice-blue eyes.

Wasn't that what Nora Roberts, her favorite romance author, once wrote about heroes who had stark blue-colored eyes like this? As much as Mary had memorized nearly every word in her favorite novels, right this moment she could barely remember her own name for sure, let alone any particular quotations.

"Um. Is that a pick-up line?" Now why was that

the first thing out of her mouth? She would scare him away.

"Maybe. But can I sit anyway?"

Oh. This guy was cool. "Sure. I might not mind being picked up tonight."

He raised his eyebrows and the corners of his mouth curved in the most interesting version of a smile that Mary had ever seen. She noticed his rugged chin then, and the even craggier jawline. His eyes were cold, deep pools. Deep and full of secrets. *Icy* was certainly the right word for them.

His black jeans and black leather jacket added to the picture of a hard man. And wasn't that a scar running from his eye to his temple?

She realized she might've been wrong. Nothing about him seemed heroic. Fascinating and handsome, maybe. But he was not a romance hero.

He reminded her of the newest actor to play James Bond. Yes, definitely. This guy looked like a secret agent.

"The name's Jake," he said as he turned to signal the waitress. "Jake Pierson."

He sat down and stuck out his hand. "And you are?"

"Mary Walsh." She took his hand and a shock wave ran up her arm.

Pulling back, she tried to look calm and pleasant instead of making a wisecrack. Wow. They had electricity between them. Just like in one of her novels. This guy was going to be *it*. For sure. She promised not to mess things up for herself.

The waitress brought Mary's wine and asked Jake for his order.

"Whatever you have on tap will be good." He gestured to Mary's wine. "And put that on my tab."

The waitress nodded and left.

"Did you just buy me a drink?" Mary's nerves were jangling with anticipation.

"That okay with you?"

"Better than okay. Thanks!" The first time a stranger had ever bought her a drink. Things were looking up.

"Tell me about yourself, Mary. What do you do and where are you from?"

"I'm a librarian in Honey Creek—unfortunately."

He chuckled and the sound warmed her down to the pit of her stomach. "Why unfortunately? I think it's great. I recently moved to Honey Creek myself."

"You did?" A man like this in her backwoods small town? Whoo boy. "Why?"

This time when he laughed out loud, the warmth flashed all the way through her body. It heated up parts of her that she'd barely known she had.

"I'm in commercial real estate. There're a couple of new projects near Honey Creek that I want to pursue."

"Really?" The possibilities for a longer-term relationship with this man danced in her mind.

She suddenly remembered that her best friend forever, Susan Kelley, had mentioned meeting a handsome new real estate agent in town. Jake must be that guy. He was sure handsome enough.

Susan had found her own true love over the past few weeks. She even had the ring to prove it. Wouldn't it be something if Mary could find someone, too?

"I don't want to talk about business." He gave her a look that seemed to be full of meaning, but she had no idea what that meaning might be. "You're not married or engaged or anything are you?"

Ohhh. *That.* "Me?" The giggle erupted before she could order it back. "Not at all."

"What's funny?"

The waitress arrived with their drink order, giving Mary a chance to think over a response. Here she was, at yet another crossroads in her life. She considered telling a white lie. Or maybe giving him a nice easy line that would avoid her having to answer. But then she remembered her father. The world's biggest liar. And she decided she hated liars and everything that went along with them. No, she had no choice but to tell Jake the truth.

If that meant that he would do a quick disappearing act—so be it.

Jake wasn't sure what he expected her to say in answer to his question. The woman acted much younger than her twenty-nine years. Perhaps she would say something about being more interested in intellectual pursuits. Or something about her current strange family circumstances.

A father who'd turned up newly dead, after having already been declared dead fifteen years ago, would probably wreak serious havoc on anyone's social life.

Whatever she would eventually say, Jake was sure enjoying the play of emotions across Mary's face while he waited. Her gorgeous eyes sidetracked him. That wondrous color hadn't shown up particularly well in the photos his partner had faxed along with her file. What hue were they exactly? What color could she possibly list for them on her driver's license?

Eyes: the color of fine aged whiskey.

Or maybe…

Eyes: deepest amber, the color of clover honey.

"For most of my life I've been at least a hundred pounds overweight," Mary finally answered flatly, with no emotion in her voice—despite what he could only describe as fear in her eyes. "I've recently taken off the weight and reached my goal…more or less."

She lowered her chin, and stared into her glass of white zinfandel before continuing, "Being the 'fat one' in every crowd tends to put people off."

"You can't be serious," he cracked, before he thought about what he was saying.

When her head came up too fast, he tried to recover. "People shouldn't judge others by their outward appearance. You're sure beautiful now. I would never have guessed you haven't always looked the same as you do now. How'd you lose the weight?"

"Are you asking if I had weight-loss surgery?" She shook her head but was watching him closely. "Too chicken. I did it the old-fashioned way—by letting a psychologist take my brain out and replace it with one a hundred pounds lighter and supposedly more sane."

A tentative chuckle leaked from her mouth, but Jake was having a hard time joining her in laughing over her little joke.

"That's phenomenal. Your willpower must be amazing." He reached over his untouched beer and took her by the hand, anxious to get even that much closer to her. "I'm impressed."

"Don't be." She tugged at her hand halfheartedly. But when he didn't let go, she stilled.

"Food was prime in my life." She reached for the wineglass with her other hand. "Dr. Fortunata helped me see the truth. For years I used food to numb and distract myself."

"Numb yourself? To what? Why would a sweet girl from a nice small town need to feel numb?"

Mary didn't want to answer him. Couldn't find the way. She made a big show of sipping wine instead.

In the meantime, familiar words kept circling through her mind. *You're no damned good, Mary Walsh. No one could ever love you. God only knows what I did to deserve a child like you. You'll always be worthless and ugly. Get out of my sight.*

"Okay," Jake said in a hoarse whisper as he rubbed his thumb across her knuckles. "Maybe that question's too personal for our very first conversation. But I like you a lot and I want to know more about you. Tell me about your family. I vaguely remember hearing something about a Walsh in the past few days... Was it on TV? A relation of yours?"

"My father." Oh, boy. If Jake hadn't run off screaming after learning she'd been a tubby all her life, finding out about her father was sure to do it.

"What happened to him?"

"They found his body. Someone murdered him." Funny, but over the years she'd gotten used to saying that word. *Murdered.* It had taken almost fifteen years, but the sound of it no longer seemed nearly as horrific as it once did.

"How awful for you. Were you two close?"

What could she say that wouldn't chase him off? Again, she had little choice but tell the truth. He was bound to find out sooner or later anyway.

"Not at all. In fact, I…everyone…thought that he'd died already. There's a fellow in the state prison doing time for murdering him fifteen years ago."

Jake sat back, but stayed in his seat. "That's…uh… unusual. Where's your father been all this time?"

She rolled her eyes and shrugged one shoulder. "Your guess would be as good as anyone's. And before you ask, I don't have a clue why he would pretend to be dead."

Probably because he was a lying playboy bastard, she thought grimly, but refused to say so. No doubt quite a few women would've been happy to see him suffer and die. Running from any of those women might've been an excellent reason for her father pretending to be dead.

Mary took a huge slug and finished off the wine. Jake motioned to the waitress again.

"I shouldn't have any more. I'm still dieting and didn't eat much today. I'm here at the librarians' conference and we've been in meetings all day." Not to mention that she normally didn't drink.

Tonight would be the first for many things, she hoped.

Jake sat back and studied her while he played with his beer mug. "You're embarrassed about your father being a murder victim. Don't be. Not unless you killed him."

"Me? I can't even step on a spider." Not that she hadn't dreamed about killing her father many times over the years. Even after she felt convinced he was already dead.

The waitress brought her another glass of wine and

Mary only stared at it as though it was a bug. Finally, she shook her head to break through her fog and picked it up. This was the start of her new life. What twenty-nine-year-old woman couldn't manage a few glasses of wine?

"My old man embarrassed the hell out of me, too, while I was growing up," Jake said, and Mary felt the tension between them easing. "He was an overbearing bastard. Bound and determined his son would grow up to be just like him—despite knowing damned well that I didn't want any part of who he was."

Mary reached out and laid a gentle hand on Jake's arm. "I'm sorry. That's hard. Who was he?"

"A survivalist. One of those crazed individuals who lives in the backwoods and stockpiles weapons, waiting for the day when the big, bad government will arrive for a showdown."

"Oh, my gosh. Sounds like an awful way to grow up." Mary's heart turned a somersault in sympathy.

"He did teach me how to handle weapons. And I can survive on my own without the trappings of civilization." Jake sounded as if he thought those things weren't any big deal.

"But that wasn't what you wanted. Was it?"

He took a swallow of what had to be by now warm beer, and then gazed at her as if she was the only person on the planet who mattered.

"Not me." With a hollow-sounding laugh, he added, "I wanted to be involved in one of civilization's biggest accomplishments—electronics. I wanted to learn how things work. How computers run. Why cell phones sometimes get signals and sometimes don't. I thought engineering was magic and I was desperate to learn all those kinds of tricks."

"Whoo boy. I bet your father hated that." Their stories weren't the same, but Mary was feeling connected to this man. A connection through their overbearing fathers.

"Yeah, he did. I got out from under his control at the first opportunity."

She took a slow sip from her glass while trying to clear her head. "So, why are you in real estate and not electronics?"

Had she slurred a couple of those words? Maybe it was time for her to give up the wine. She set the glass back down on the table and tried to focus her eyes on Jake.

He wiped his hand across his forehead and then put his palm out as if he was unable to explain himself.

After a moment he said, "Commercial real estate is more lucrative. Electronics makes a better hobby."

He'd opted for the money. Of course. She could certainly understand that. She was considering a change of jobs for the very same reason.

"You're not married?" Jeez. She must be drunk.

"I've never had the pleasure." His whole expression changed and he smiled as if she'd just handed him the moon—or a new BlackBerry. "So far, I haven't found anyone who could love me."

Think of that. They were like two nuts off the same branch. Mary felt as if she'd known him all her life.

The waitress arrived at the table. "Sorry. It's closing time. The bartender says you can have one more round. But you'll need to drink up."

Jake turned to Mary and inclined his head as though it were totally up to her.

"No, thanks. I think I've had my limit."

After the waitress took Jake's money and left, Mary began to rise from her seat and said, "I can't believe it's 1:00 a.m. already. I...wish we had more time to talk."

Talking wasn't what she wanted, but she didn't have the foggiest notion of how to ask him back to her room.

Jake jumped up from the table and helped her to her feet. "Let's take our time going back to your room. We can talk on the way."

Trying her best to keep the wide-eyed look of wonder off her face, she knew she was failing miserably. But she couldn't help it. Everything she had ever wanted—ever dreamed about—was right here beside her.

And he was walking her back to her room.

Chapter 2

Jake's mission couldn't have been going any better if he'd written his target's lines himself. After a couple of hours and several glasses of wine, he'd already piqued Mary's interest enough that she'd allowed him to walk her back to her room. This night would be a great start to his plan—of becoming Mary's boyfriend.

When she weaved from side to side down the hall, he slid his arm around her shoulders. She trembled slightly under the weight of his arm. Taking a deep breath, he caught the sweet smell of strawberries coming from her hair. A perfect scent for her. Like a field full of summer sunshine.

It made him want to pull her closer. Take her in his arms and kiss her until they both lost track of their senses. Until the smell of strawberries surrounded them in a cloud of lust.

Ahem. *The mission always comes first.*

Straightening up, he went over the things bothering him about this assignment—in addition to his unusual physical reactions to the target. The target—Mary. He'd never met anyone quite as guileless as she seemed. Like a naive teen, she appeared incapable of holding back or fudging the truth. Was it all an act? To his trained lawman's eye she looked about as old as the twenty-nine that was listed as her age. Those minor laugh wrinkles at the corners of her eyes gave her away.

If she was putting on a gullible act for some reason, she sure as hell had him suckered in. But he was supposed to be a pro. This was his twelfth mission in ten years. Not his first.

Still, this mission marked the first time that he had actually given out his own background during an undercover operation. Not a smart move. Once a covert agent started mixing up his cover story with his own life history, the whole backstory he'd constructed might come crumbling down around him. He understood that well.

But she had been completely open with him about her relationship to her father. Open and embarrassed about letting him see that the murdered man was not someone she was sorry to see dead. Mark Walsh must've been difficult for her to deal with during their years together.

Jake thought about how a good covert agent twisted with the wind. Went with the flow. The truth about his own father had come tumbling from his lips in an effort to gain her sympathy. Then he'd had a hell of a time recovering when she'd asked him why he'd chosen to go into real estate.

Real estate. Why had he ever allowed Jim to talk him into that crazy cover? Yeah, yeah. Jake understood how real estate would be the perfect occupation, allowing a man on a mission to gain information. Real estate gave him plenty of excuses for snooping around. *Just looking for potential property acquisitions.*

But now, hell…

"We're almost there."

They were. A few more doors down the hall. And they had yet to say two words to each other on the way here.

Jake checked over his shoulder, still concerned that the earlier attack on him had some connection to his mission. But the hotel hallway was quiet. Not one soul in sight. His gut told him they were as isolated out in the hall as they would be inside her room.

Mary pulled the key card from her purse and stopped. She turned to him with the most hopeful expression on her face.

"This is it."

She was beautiful. Her eyes sparkled with youthful anticipation. Her long, full hair dared him to run his hands through it—to lose himself in the satiny texture and heavenly scent. But could he stoop to taking improper advantage of her inebriated state? It wouldn't be fair.

The mission always comes first.

It had been eons since she'd let a man kiss her, and in Mary's memory those previous times had been… stressful. She'd wondered why she had ever thought to give it a second try.

But wasn't that why she'd come to Bozeman in the first place?

She gazed up into Jake's piercing blue eyes and saw a sizzle in them that made her all antsy and suddenly filled with unbearable longing. *Oh, yeah.* She was going to try kissing a man again. Now. Right now.

He bent his head, came within a whisper of her mouth and hesitated. It seemed as if he was giving her a chance to back out. Not a prayer of that happening.

Mary closed the gap between them and fell into heaven. Instead of his mouth being mashed to hers as had happened in her previous experiences, Jake toyed with her lips. He nipped at them, then licked his tongue across her bottom lip to soothe any small pain. The tip of his tongue touched the middle of her closed mouth tentatively as if he wanted her to open up for him.

She parted her lips, let his tongue enter and experienced pure bliss. He dug his fingers through her thick hair and pulled her closer. All of a sudden, the languorousness that had begun in her chest and tummy widened to encompass her limbs. Her fingers grew warm and limp. Her legs became weak and shaky.

As he tightened his hold she felt every inch of his hard body pressed against her softness. His erection pushed into her belly. A jolt zapped through her when she came to the amazing realization that she was the one making him hot. Outstanding.

Their tongues tangled again and the sensual awareness inside her grew to impossible heights. Her whole body began tingling. This was how a kiss was supposed to be. She'd read all about kisses and knew that at least some people liked the feelings that went along with a really good kiss. But she'd never imagined it could be like this.

Letting herself revel in the sensations, she noted the changes in her body's temperature. From somewhere in the back of her mind she knew that sweat was starting to form at her temples. Her palms were becoming damp. Her panties were getting wet between her thighs.

The key card slipped from her fingers and hit the carpet.

"Oh." She pulled her head back and then bent to pick up the key, but her knees refused to hold her up. "Oh."

Crumbling to the floor, she felt flushed with embarrassment and regret. Surely no other woman had ever collapsed after their very best kiss ever and before they'd even made it to the bed. How ridiculous that she could be this much of a newbie at her age.

"You okay?" He reached out his hand to help her up.

"Um. I guess so." If *okay* meant having the most amazing kiss of her whole life.

She tried to stand, but found her legs wouldn't hold her up. "I can't… I can't…" Down she went again, landing on her backside.

When she began to laugh and cry at the same time, Jake took pity on her and reached down to haul her up in his arms. After all, it was his fault that she'd had too much to drink. He'd wanted her talking and in a good mood—not too drunk to stand up.

But he would never in a million years regret that kiss.

"The key card," she said through giggles and tears.

His knees were almost too old for this kind of move,

but he managed to hang on to her and at the same time bend to pick up the card.

"I've got it." He opened the door and brushed them both inside.

Once inside he was at a loss for what to do with her. He didn't figure she was in any shape to stand on her own two feet again. Her room was small. One queen-size bed. One nightstand and one dresser with a TV sitting on top. The lone chair in the room was shoved into a far corner under a minuscule desk. Straight-backed with no cushions, he couldn't figure a way to place her upright in that chair without her sliding back to the floor.

Sighing, Jake walked to the bed and lowered her gently to a sitting position on the mattress. Steadying her, he stepped back and watched, making sure she didn't hit the floor again.

She popped straight up like a Whac-A-Mole. He pushed at her shoulders until she went down on the bed again. She came right back up.

"Hey, aren't you going to kiss me again?" She took a shaky step in his direction.

He took another step backward toward the door. "I think I'd better be going."

"Not just yet." She grinned at him and his whole body went rock-hard. "Um…um… Stay long enough to help me."

He would be a lot better off simply making a run for the door; instead, Jake made the fatal mistake of asking, "Help you with what?"

Rocking uneasily on her feet, she reached for the hem of her sparkly orange, long-sleeved top and pulled it up and over her head in one move. Pitching the top into a corner, she turned back to him wearing nothing above the waist but a silky lace bra and a big smile. She tilted her head and stared at him as if to say, *Help me and yourself, big boy.*

"Do you know what you're doing?" His voice was too steely and harsh for the situation. But he was at a loss as to how to change things.

She shook her head. "What am I doing?"

"Making it hotter than hell in here." His mind was on a dangerous edge as he fought with dueling impulses. He needed an out. Fast. Or an excuse to change the subject.

Fortunately, he'd spotted something to talk about while she'd had her back turned. It gave him a momentary reprieve and would be something to occupy her mind, he hoped.

"You have a tattoo on your shoulder." He slid a little farther away and pointed. "What is that? A mermaid?"

"That's Disney's Ariel. I had her done last week. I think she's kinda sexy. Do you like her?"

The mermaid tattoo did look like a kid's cartoon character. It was sweet, but not the least bit sexy.

"She looks like you," he managed. "With the red hair and all. But why her?"

"The tattoo was an effort to change. To become a new person."

That sounded like just so much psycho babble to him. "And did you? Become a new person?"

Mary's face flushed bright red. "Not yet. But Ariel is helping me on my journey to find the real me. I was hoping…" Her words stopped as her face paled.

Reaching a shaking hand toward him, she clutched

her stomach with the other hand. "I was hoping you would help me, too."

With that, whatever she'd eaten for the past twenty-four hours came back up her throat and spewed from her mouth. If he'd been a step closer, it would've gone all over him. As it was, the goo covered her pants and got on her shoes.

She started to cry in earnest. "I'm sooo sorry. Look at me. I'm a mess."

"Don't worry. I'll help." He couldn't stop himself. He could no more leave her like this than he could play the violin. It wasn't in him.

He took great care in carrying Mary into the bathroom and cleaning her up. After using a washcloth on her face, he splashed water into her mouth and let her swish toothpaste to rinse. When he was done, he helped her out of her shoes and pants and pitched them into the tub. He found a couple of aspirin in her bag on the back of the toilet and got them down her with a big glass of water. Then he carted her to the bed, threw the covers back and slid her between the sheets.

"Thank you. I'm grateful. But my head is still spinning." She beamed up at him. "Are you going to join me?"

He shook his head and saw the shadow of disappointment cross her face. "Uh, I'd better clean up some more before I do anything else."

"Don't leave me, Jake. Please."

"I won't go far," he promised. "You're going to be fine. Don't worry. Rest is what you need most."

It took him ten minutes to wet a couple of towels and clean up the carpeting. He threw the towels into the tub and filled it up with hot water to let everything soak.

When he arrived back beside the bed, Mary was sound asleep. He headed for the door. With his hand on the knob, he remembered his promise not to leave.

But she would be all right. He could sneak out and she would never notice he'd left until morning.

Then he made the mistake of turning back to look at her.

She looked peaceful now, but what if she had alcohol poisoning or something? Perhaps she could get sick again and choke to death before ever waking up.

He walked to the desk and dragged the tiny chair over beside the bed. Figuring he could sit here for a while, he decided he had nothing better to do tonight.

As Jake stared down into Mary's sweet face, he remembered their kiss. He'd kissed a lot of women over the years. In fact, for five whole years of his life he had looked forward to sharing his wife's kisses on a daily basis. But Tina had been gone for ten years, and at this point he couldn't quite bring the memory of his dead wife's kisses to mind anymore.

Was that disloyal? Jake couldn't stand thinking about that possibility, or about Tina right now.

He couldn't concentrate on anything but the way Mary clung to him. The way her body had melded to his as if the two of them were destined to be together. As if they had been made for each other right from the beginning of time.

A stray curl of soft red hair had fallen over her cheek, and he reached over to push it behind her ear. Running his knuckles over ivory skin, Jake remembered how open she'd been. From the very beginning in the bar, she'd been willing to tell him anything.

She'd also been wide-open to his kisses. Gave him

everything he asked for—and more. She was a hell of a good kisser, making him wonder who had taught her so well. Her file hadn't listed a boyfriend or fiancé, but Jake felt sure that by the age of twenty-nine there must've been someone.

The thought of her file reminded Jake of his mission. He wouldn't leave her for long, but he was overdue to check in with his partner.

Forcing his fingers away from her soft, smooth skin, Jake pulled the sheet up over her shoulders and tucked her in. He'd covered up the mermaid, but he didn't think she would mind.

Smiling, he pocketed her key card and slipped out of the room. Seconds later he was down the outside stairs and in the parking lot, looking for a quiet place to make his call.

"What do you mean your assailant—the *kid*—got away?" His partner Jim was chuckling so loudly over the phone that Jake was afraid someone in the hotel might be able to hear him. "You can't mean you've suddenly grown into such an old man."

Stepping farther under a tall ponderosa pine, Jake gritted his teeth and backed into the shadows. "Ha. Ha. Very funny. What are you? All of two years younger than I am? Or maybe you've regressed to your teenage years while I've been away. At least I got in a clean shot at the kid. Broke his nose for sure."

"If he was someone from Honey Creek, a broken nose won't be hard to spot." Jim's silent grin shouted right through the receiver, even though he made every effort to hide it by clearing his throat. "How about the target? Mary Walsh. How'd your first contact go?"

Jake had to bite his tongue. No way would he tell his partner how unprofessional he'd been.

"Fine," he said in a calm voice. "The new plan is going to work out great. In a couple of days I should be meeting everyone in town through her."

Before Jim could ask anything else about Mary, Jake sent the conversation off in a slightly different direction. "I know the sheriff in Honey Creek is your old navy SEAL buddy, but are you sure he is definitely in the clear on the murder of our informant?"

"Wes Colton is so straight you could mistake him for a ruler." Jim took a deep breath through his nose and Jake could imagine him tempering his irritation over the insolent question. "Wes isn't involved in our money-laundering investigation. You and I already came to that conclusion. He's provided us with solid information."

Jake tsked at his partner's lame excuses. "We're talking about the murder of our main informant. You do remember that we've discussed the fact that Mark Walsh had a lot of enemies? His death could've been a crime of passion and not connected to our investigation at all. There're several kinds of passion. Revenge, for one. Wes Colton's brother has been sitting in the Montana State Prison for the past fifteen years for a crime he obviously did not commit. Sounds like a possible motive for murder to me."

Jim grunted through the phone. "I've already checked on Wes's whereabouts around the time of Mark Walsh's murder, smart-ass. He was at Quantico, taking one of the Bureau's weekend classes for local enforcement. He was back in time to haul the body out of the creek. But as a suspect? Nope, he's not a possibility. Check the sheriff off your list."

This time it was Jake who was holding back the chuckle. "Got it. Anything else?"

"Dead ends and false leads so far. But I'm working every detail. Keep me informed of how you're doing in Honey Creek."

Jake hung up and pocketed his phone. Taking one more exploratory trip around the hotel grounds, he checked for anything suspicious and came up empty.

He headed back to Mary's room, hoping she hadn't awakened while he'd been gone. After he'd slipped inside and checked to make sure she was still breathing, he emptied the bathtub and wrung out the towels. Mary's clothes looked like a lost cause. He dumped them in a pile on the floor.

Then Jake took up residence in the straight-backed desk chair. One of the most uncomfortable places to sit in his memory.

But he kicked off his shoes and settled down to wait anyway. He wanted to watch her until the morning to assure himself that she was okay.

While he watched her sleeping, Jake vowed that he would use these hours to his best advantage. He would work to convince himself that the two of them *could* indeed have a romantic relationship without becoming intimate. He vowed to use her only up to a point. After all, a few things in life went far beyond his job description.

"No. No. No. Don't make me."

Jake practically jumped out of his seat and scanned the room for intruders. Early-morning light peeked around the edges of the curtains. No intruders.

Another noise drew his attention toward the bed.

Mary was whimpering and flailing her arms in her sleep. Tears streamed down her cheeks, and she cried out with unintelligible words.

"I hate you. Hate you!" Those words had been clear enough. He relaxed slightly, realizing she was having a nightmare.

In the next moment she twisted in her sheets and kicked fiercely. She screamed and he began to worry that she was becoming hysterical and might hurt herself. Mary then uttered words that drove a chill up Jake's spine and sent him stumbling to her side.

"I wish you were dead. I swear I'll kill you!"

Chapter 3

Strong arms closed around her, bringing Mary out of her nightmare with a start. *Where was she? And who could be jumping her while she slept?*

"Easy there. Everything's okay. I've got you. It was only a bad dream."

Jake. The cobwebs in her mind disappeared in a flash and she pasted herself to his body. If it had been possible to crawl right inside him, she would not have hesitated.

He cocooned her. Wrapped her in warmth and tenderness.

"Relax," he whispered into her hair. "You're safe."

Swallowing down the night's terrors, Mary reached out toward his face to assure herself that this was no dream. She used her forefinger to trace his features, drawing a line from his high forehead down his Roman nose. Her fingers fanned across the strength in his jaw and in and out of the tiny cleft in his chin. She wanted to memorize every dip and ridge, every nuance.

The reality of being in bed with a sexy man was so much better than anything she had ever read in the pages of a book. She molded herself to him—tried to align their legs in perfect union.

His breathing became rough, uneven. She heard and it turned her to mush. She fisted her hands in his shirt and breathed in his exotic smell. All man. Masculine and exhilarating.

Jake eased back and gently rubbed his thumbs across her wet cheeks. "Okay? No more dream bad guys?"

More than okay, she felt totally wonderful. As though someone had poured a vat of warm chocolate over her. This was what she had been waiting for her whole entire lifetime.

He bent his head and placed his lips against her forehead. Nuh-uh. Not what she wanted from him at all.

Digging her hands in his hair, she pulled his head back and put his lips where she wanted them. On hers. Her tongue slid inside his mouth. The all-consuming flames instantly sprang between them, as she'd expected—as she'd hoped.

Sensation after sensation raged through her. Rainbows of bright colors. Textures and shapes, a tapestry of passion.

Frantic to touch him—everywhere—Mary kept half her brain concentrating on the taste of his mouth and on worrying his lips between her own. And with the other half of her fuzzy mind, she fought to open the buttons on his shirt. A button popped. Then something ripped. But the sounds only served to spur her on.

At last she reached her goal, warm skin and chest hair. The sensation of wiry hair against her fingertips was erotic. She wanted to plant her lips there, replacing her fingers. She needed a taste of him. Of all of him. The pulse right below the surface at the base of his neck would be a great place to start. His salty skin and all those fascinating hidden ridges and creases came next.

"You're killing me here." He dragged his mouth from hers, panting hard.

Through his sensual haze, Jake knew his breathing wasn't the only thing growing hard. She was too close. He couldn't think. Couldn't remember why they shouldn't be doing this.

"Am I hurting you?"

Exasperated, Jake pried her fingers off his shirt and placed her hand against the hard ridge lying under the zipper of his pants. "What do you think?"

"Oh." Her voice was deep, flirty. "Then don't stop now."

Before he could stop her, she began lowering his zipper. The sound mesmerized him. Like someone scratching their way out of a dilemma. His every sense went on alert. The feel of her luxurious hair against his skin. The sound of her breathing coming from her mouth in small pants. When she looked up into his eyes, he saw fire.

He felt something inside him clutch, then give way. He'd seen her willingness. Her longing. Through her sensitive touch he'd found she not only had gentleness and passion, but empathy as well.

It had been a long damned time since he'd wanted anything—anyone this badly.

His erection popped free. Mary sighed deeply and took him in hand. Her obvious pleasure at touching him was contagious. He rolled her to her back and ran his hands down her rib cage and up to cup her breasts.

Her mouth brushed over his briefly, setting fires where she kissed. Just enough to burn through any of his remaining boundaries. He covered her mouth and kissed her back relentlessly. Her lips and tongue stoked the flames of his desire and burned any questions or regrets away like so many cinders blowing in the wind.

"Mary." A single word. A single breath.

And he was lost.

The blood coursed through his veins, leaving his brain and rushing to his extremities. He was out of control. Defenseless against his own needs.

Desperate, he slid her arms free of the bra, pulled it to her waist and then filled his hands with her lush flesh. Her breasts were firm and as soft as rose petals. As he thumbed over the nubby tips, her chest rose and fell. She moaned through pursed lips. His fingers had found perfection, but his mouth hungered for its turn.

He lowered his head to take what he wanted. When his mouth closed over the hard and pebbled peak of one breast, she arched upward with a gasp. Pulling her deeper into his mouth, he laved his tongue back and forth over her nipple. It grew harder—and so did he.

Ignoring the growing ache in his groin, he kept his attention focused on Mary, on her reactions to his moves. As he moved to the other breast, she whimpered and moved restlessly under him. He took a nip of the tip, just a tiny bite. She jumped but made it clear she liked what he was doing, digging her fingernails into his shoulders and holding him right where she wanted. Blowing air over her to both soothe and stir, he kissed and suckled her breasts until she begged.

"Jake, *please*. I want…I want…"

Yes, Jake knew what she wanted and was determined to please them both. Why he shouldn't seemed lost in a haze of need and desire.

He flattened the palm of his hand on her belly and felt her muscles quivering under his touch. Inching his fingers beneath her panties, he soon reached his goal— all that glorious heat in the lush curls at the center of her thighs. He brushed aside any silky material standing in his path. With her help he pulled the undergarment down and off, frantic that nothing should stand between them.

He shoved his own slacks out of the way with one hand while he used the other to stroke and torture. Her thighs fell open and she lifted her hips off the bed. Finding her already wet and hot, he bent his head and dipped his tongue into her sweetness.

Mary groaned, struggled and urged him back up her body. He obliged her, blazing kisses over her belly and across the valleys and curves of her body. Then she reached down and gripped him with both her hands, using a gentle touch that drove him wild.

He jerked and went rigid. Her touch ruled his moves. But he didn't want gentle from her. His whole body felt like molten lava and Jake knew he couldn't last much longer. He grabbed her wrists and pulled her hands up over her head.

Looking into her face, he found her glazed eyes fixed

on him. "Now, Jake," she said through a sob. "I beg you. Hurry."

She lifted her hips, inviting him inside. With a last bit of clarity, he reached into his pants pocket for his wallet. He found the silver-wrapped condom and had it freed and installed within seconds.

Moving over her again, he let the tip of his erection nudge her swollen flesh. She writhed. Whimpered. He leaned his hips forward, brushing his length against her for a second time while she cried out her pleasure.

The sound enflamed him, engulfed him, as blood pulsed and pooled in the part of him begging for quick release. His own ragged breathing blocked the tiny niggles of guilt already building deep inside his chest.

When he brushed her entrance for a third time, she bucked upward. Her whole body pleaded for him as she rubbed herself against his length and called out his name. Every inch of her wept with wanting, and she begged him to hurry.

With amazing self-control, Jake gently pressed his hard length inside her entrance. Testing. He needed this to be good for her. Better for her than for him.

Her internal opening surrounded him with tiny tremors. Like welcome-home hugs. Hearing her making explicit noises of pleasure, he pressed a little deeper into the shock waves. But he wanted her to be just as wild with need as he was. With some regret he made a slow withdrawal, only seconds later to inch forward again.

She tensed but murmured encouragement. Her body was like a warm, welcoming paradise, tight and wet. The greatest gift he'd ever been offered. He pushed deeper, trying not to rush.

Feeling her body start to contract around him, he slid himself farther toward ecstasy. So hot. Slick. Tight.

Just before he succumbed to the madness, it hit him. *Too tight.* There might not be any barrier, but no one had ever come this way before. He suddenly knew for certain that he was the first.

Her first? Was it possible?

He used the last bit of his resolve to lean up on his elbows and look down at her. Her face was the picture of abandon. Her hair a wild carpet spread out across the pillows.

This was too big a gift for him to take without words. "Mary."

Not sure he could stop if she asked him to, he still felt he had to try. Had to say something.

She'd closed her eyes and arched her neck, pushing her engorged breasts up invitingly. He tried not to look. Fought to forget their sweet taste.

"Mary, listen to me." Desperation colored his efforts.

"Please. Please. Please." She undulated her hips and threw her legs over his thighs, bringing him closer to the edge.

"Mary, look at me."

Her head swung back and forth. Her arms went around his back, trying to urge him down into her. He wanted what she seemed to want. To slam his body into hers and bring them to the quick ending they both craved. Why did he hesitate? It was a hell of a time for another attack of conscience, but he was already up to his ears in guilt. He had to keep trying to make her listen.

Jake fisted his hands in her hair and forced her

attention. "Are you sure? Sure it's me you want? You don't even know me."

She stared up at him with heavy-lidded eyes, her lips slightly parted and her chest heaving. His mouth went dry as she bit on her bottom lip and tried to smile.

"Time doesn't matter. I know you," she managed on a hoarse laugh. "I chose you because you're a good person. A kind and careful soul who cares about being somebody's first."

Jake started to shake his head, to deny what she'd said. He was far removed from anyone who resembled such a description. But she didn't know it. Couldn't know it.

Her internal canal began convulsing around him, milking him and seducing him to complete the lesson. "Mary. Damn it. I can't do this."

"Shush. Jake, please. I'm so close to something and I know it's going to be spectacular. Please…"

She didn't have time to complete her plea because Jake gave in to the temptation jolting through him. Dripping with sweat, he thrust hard into her and embedded himself to the hilt. He couldn't think. Could only let go.

Could only cry out when he felt the contractions take her and she screamed his name in pleasure. He pumped hard into each one of her rolling earthquakes.

Faster and faster. Higher and higher. Until they were each a sobbing, shouting explosion.

As one, they shuddered and fell over the edge. Together in body—if not in mind.

Amazing.

Sprawled over the bed, tangled in Jake's arms and

legs, Mary waited for her heart rate to slow. She couldn't move. Didn't want to.

Unbelievable. Utterly unbelievable.

Why hadn't she known about this before? But then again, she hadn't met Jake before now. Grateful. Yes, totally grateful that she'd waited for him, she turned her head to make sure he was all right. His skin was damp, glistening with sweat. And his breathing was as erratic as her own.

"Thank God," she murmured.

Jake opened his eyes and rolled to look at her. "For what?"

"Thank God you were the first."

He shifted to one side, pulled her snugly against him and pressed a kiss to her hair. "You could've told me."

She laid a palm on his chest, felt the pulse beat of his heart. "What? That I was a twenty-nine-year-old virgin? And how long would you have stuck around after hearing that?"

His chuckle rumbled up through her hand. "Maybe you're right. And I would've hated missing what just happened here."

"See? I have a lot of strikes against me. And I wanted you. Badly."

"I wanted you from the first moment I laid eyes on you." He kissed the tip of her nose, then raised her hand to his lips and kissed her fingertips. "I saw you in that sparkly orange top and nearly swallowed my tongue."

"It's burnt umber, not orange. Red-haired women aren't supposed to wear orange." But this red-haired woman was going to wear that top as much as possible from now on.

She started to turn over but winced with the discovery that lots of interesting places on her body ached.

Jake's mouth pressed into a hard line. "I didn't even manage to get your bra all the way off. Hell of a way for a first time to go."

He rolled out of bed, ripped off his own rumpled shirt and then reached back and undid her bra. She started to follow him to her feet, but he put his hand down and held her still.

"Hold on. I know what you need right now." He slid his hands under her body and lifted her into his arms. "Let me take care of you."

Feeling like a princess, like her little mermaid, Mary grinned into his shoulder as she threw her arms around his neck and hung on.

He carried her into the bathroom and stepped with her into the bathtub. Then he turned on the shower tap, thankfully warm. The spray covered them in a shower of liquid calm.

Slowly, Jake lowered her down his body to stand on her own shaky legs. "Hang there a second." He kept one arm tightly around her and reached for the soap. "You're going to find out that good sex is always messy, Miss Mary Ariel."

"I like the sound of that. I wish my parents had called me Ariel. Maybe I'll change my name." Along with her whole life—starting tonight.

He placed a wet kiss on the mermaid's face and Mary laughed, feeling careless and coy.

The bar of soap rubbing across her breasts made her nipples tighten. Did he notice? Jake never changed the motion. His knuckles brushed the soft undersides of her breasts. He ran his hands down her spine and around her backside. He seemed intent on smoothing soap bubbles over her skin and she wasn't sure he was paying attention.

Until…he reached between her legs. His touch was as light as a cloud, and he bent his head to place gentle lips against her wet temple.

An electric buzz rushed through her veins like a warm wind. Desire, close to the surface since their first kiss, kicked off her pulse again. Her heart pounded with the need, the heat.

"Jake…" The word was only a whisper of sound. A plea. A question.

But it didn't have the desired effect.

He pulled his hand away and stepped back, studying her under the spray. Suddenly she felt more embarrassed than she had in her whole life and raised both palms to cover her breasts. No man had ever seen her stark naked before. It was one thing to have sex in bed—in the dark. It was quite another to be faced with full-frontal nudity under the bathroom's fluorescent light.

Jake's eyes clouded over and instead of ice blue, they looked gray and unfocused. "That's it." He handed her the soap, turned his back and pushed aside the shower curtain ready to step out of the tub.

"Is it me?" she asked quietly. "Now that you've seen me in the light are you regretting what we did?"

He shook his head, then turned back and reached for her. "Maybe I have some guilt. But I'll never regret one moment of what we did. Don't ever think that. You are a gorgeous woman. And if I had a choice…"

Pulling her close, he lasered a kiss across her lips. A kiss that spoke of need and desperation. A kiss that spoke of *tomorrow*.

By the time he let her go, his breathing was coming in hard pants and his erection was poking her in the stomach. "You're going to be sore for a couple of days. You have lots of time left in your future to experience everything. Let's take things slow for now."

She sighed but nodded her acceptance of his decision. It wasn't her first choice but if he could wait, so could she.

Jake stepped from the tub. "Take your time. When you get out we'll have breakfast before we each head back to Honey Creek."

He put a towel over the bar for her to use after the shower. "This is the only dry cloth left in the room, and it's all yours. I'll air-dry. Oh, and when you get out of the shower, you might want to make a decision about your clothes."

"My...?"

He grinned and pointed to the pile by the sink.

"My new silk pants? And my brand-new heels? They look ruined." The pants would probably be easy to replace, though she regretted the heels.

"Sorry you picked last night to wear your new clothes."

"*All* my clothes are new." Hmm. That sounded a little too sharp and full of self-pity and it wasn't how she truly felt. "Besides, those clothes were lucky for me."

"I told you never to call me here."

At the same time as Mary was stepping from the shower, Truman was making lame excuses.

"But, boss, I'm using a pay phone outside the Bozeman hospital E.R. No one will find out."

The boss tried to keep sudden anger and frustration

from spilling over through the phone. "I'm not paying you to get your nose broken. I wanted you to follow that new guy around for a while and report back on his behavior. What's the idea of jumping him?"

Groaning, Truman raced to explain, "He looked like he was spying on somebody. I only wanted to scare him off. Make him regret he came to our part of the country."

"Yeah? And that worked out so well, didn't it?"

"It's not my fault." Truman's whining voice set nerves to jangling. "He's gotta be some kind of pro."

The idea wasn't a novel one. "I'm beginning to believe you're right. I thought at first he was a private investigator and I wanted to know who hired him. I'm more convinced now that he's probably a fed. DEA or FBI maybe. Makes me think I'd better bring in a pro myself."

Truman issued a laugh, but the sound rang hollow and too loud across the line. "You get him, boss. What do you want me to do next?"

"Go on vacation."

"But, boss…"

"Get out of the area. Go to Florida for a while. I don't want to see your face around here until your nose heals. Is that clear?"

If it wasn't clear, the boss figured the pro he hired could take care of Truman the same way as he would take care of the undercover agent in their midst.

Permanently.

Chapter 4

"Ow!" Mary rammed her hip into the book cart for the third time this morning.

Darn it. Why couldn't she watch where she was going? After all, she'd been employed as the assistant librarian here at the Honey Creek library for the past eight years. Certainly by now she should know where everything was located.

Absolutely nothing had been going right. Not since she and Jake had parted ways last Saturday morning in the parking lot of the Bozeman hotel. That morning had been so hopeful—so full of promise. They'd exchanged cell phone numbers and had stolen a few public kisses.

He'd said he would call. But her friend Susan told her that was what they all said.

Not in romance novels. In her favorite books the

couples might have their troubles, but things always worked out in the end. If a hero said he would do something, he did it. The heroic characters she'd read about in romance novels were what had given her the idea that a man could be trusted.

Not that she'd had many examples of that in real life.

Nothing her father had ever said was the truth. He'd cheated on her mother. He'd probably cheated his business partners and friends. He'd even cheated about his own death.

Jake was not like her father. Yet Jake had said he would call, and here it was a rainy Tuesday morning and no word yet.

Why couldn't she get over what had happened between them? Yes, he'd been her first lover and she knew a woman's first was supposedly a big deal. But this yearning to make love to him all over again seemed to have put her under a spell. A strong and unyielding spell. Was that natural? Being reckless wasn't like her. Or at least not like the person she used to be.

If she could just see him again… Maybe she would discover that he wasn't everything she remembered. Maybe…

A squeal of delight coming from the children's book section caught Mary's attention. She started walking that way to find out which book had enthralled the little girl.

One of the biggest changes Mary wanted to make in her life was having kids. She wanted one, or maybe two—or three. Now that she'd lost the weight and it was possible to think about such things, it seemed children were on her mind a lot.

As she passed by the computer stations, empty at this hour, she fought the urge to stop and look up Jake Pierson. To check up on his background. But she would never do that without telling him first. It seemed dishonest.

"Mary, may I speak to you a moment?" Mrs. Banks, the head librarian, motioned from her office.

Mary changed course and headed her way. She'd been meaning to have a serious conversation with her boss for the past couple of days. Ever since she'd decided to change her whole life. But, well, the time had never seemed quite right.

Mrs. Banks ushered her into the tiny office and shut the door behind them. "Have a seat, Mary. I'd like to tell you something. My husband has decided to retire from his job and he wants us to move to Arizona. He likes the weather there."

"No kidding?" Mary couldn't imagine living anywhere else but Honey Creek. This was home. All her family and friends were here, along with everything else she knew and loved.

Mrs. Banks put her hand up as if she was about to say something profound. "I gave three weeks' notice to the Library Board last night. They asked me to suggest my replacement."

Mary began shaking her head before her boss even finished her thought.

Mrs. Banks must've noticed the denial in Mary's expression because she gave her the cordial smile of a long-time business comrade. "I know you don't have the credentials, Mary. But if you really want the job, I'll go to bat for you."

Mary's boss had been her mentor from the beginning,

and Mrs. Banks must've assumed Mary wanted what she wanted. She did not.

"You could always get your master's degree in Library Science while you worked," Mrs. Banks added. "It'll be difficult to accomplish both at the same time in this small town, but it's possible."

"Thanks." Mary's mouth rushed to say something else, but her mind was lagging as she fought to find the right words. "But…I… I've been meaning to tell you… I've been thinking about quitting myself."

Mrs. Banks raised eyebrows expressed what she thought of that idea. "You don't want to work at the library anymore? What will you do?"

Good question. One Mary had been mulling over for weeks. "I have a few ideas. But I was hoping for a little time to check things out."

"Does this have anything to do with the authorities finding your father's body last week?"

"No." And that was the truth. Her father had nothing whatever to do with her wanting to make some changes. After all, she'd lost over a hundred pounds on her own— before his body had been found for the second time.

"I see. Then I can tell the board to look for someone else?"

Mary nodded, but bowed her head rather than face the disappointment in Mrs. Banks's eyes.

"Okay then. A young woman who used to live in Honey Creek recently contacted me about a job." Mrs. Banks's expression was thoughtful. "I'll check on her qualifications. In the meantime, Mary, if you need a few days off, the best time would be during the next couple of weeks. While I'm still here and can watch over a temp."

Mary agreed to take time off, starting tomorrow, and then she left her boss's office as quickly as possible. Now she'd done it. Big changes would be coming at her fast. Whether she was ready for them or not.

Outside the Honey Creek library at 5:00 p.m. on a drizzly Tuesday evening, Jake leaned against his rental SUV and waited for Mary to get off work.

Torn between duty and his awakening feelings for Mary, Jake had spent the better part of four days secretly meeting with the Honey Creek sheriff and assuring himself that Mary had absolutely nothing to do with Wes's current murder investigation. Somewhere along the line, Jake had found himself hoping he'd been totally wrong about Mary and that she was the murderer. That notion would be infinitely better than the idea of her as an innocent bystander that he was using for his investigation.

But no. Mary was exactly what she seemed.

Sweet. Naive. Trusting. And no longer a virgin, due to his asinine lack of self-control.

A trickle of cold summer rain eased down the back of Jake's neck, but he shook it off. He deserved to stand in a frozen hell for what he'd done to Mary—for what he intended to do.

His head came up when he spotted her at the library's front door. She was opening an umbrella and making her way down the stairs past the building's wide white columns.

Damn, but she was pretty. Even wet and dressed in a plain gray dress that seemed suitable only for a librarian. The sight of her made things twist inside him, and that hadn't happened in a very long time.

Folding his arms over his chest, he waited for her to come closer. It was starting to register in his idiot's mind that Mary might be in real danger. Honey Creek had at least one murderer lurking about. And Jake's gut was telling him that whether or not Mark Walsh's death and his own money-laundering investigation were linked, one murder could easily become two.

He'd been trying to narrow down the possible suspects, but found it difficult without knowing the people involved. He'd come to the conclusion that the best plan was to meet the various townsfolk. Maybe he could gain access to a couple of their personal computers and files.

And what better way to accomplish those goals than in the company of a beautiful, sexy woman—who might be in need of a protector?

But he swore there would be no more intimate nights. No more erotic touches and starry-eyed kisses. His conscience couldn't take it.

"Jake?" Mary stood a few feet away in the rain, staring up at him. "What are you doing here?" Her eyes were the color of a pale ale today and clouded with questions.

He wished he could give them to her. "Waiting for you. And hoping you'll come to dinner with me."

"That would be nice. But where have you—"

Gathering her in his arms, he rushed her around the car and seated her in the passenger seat before she could change her mind—or ask any difficult questions. He didn't want to give her a chance to think too much. Not about dinner. And especially not about him.

By the time he'd slipped behind the driver's wheel,

she was buckling up and placing her wet umbrella on the floor mats under her feet.

He turned the ignition key and brought the car to life. "I thought we'd go to Kelley's Cookhouse for barbecue. That okay with you?"

Out of the corner of his eye, he caught her rolling her eyes before she asked, "You sure that's where you want to go? My best friend's family owns the place and we're likely to run into everyone in town I know."

He'd already started the car, but now he put it into neutral and stepped on the brake. "Mary...Ariel..." He reached over, captured her hand and tried a sincere smile. "I want to meet your friends and family. I want us to learn everything there is to know about each other. Give me a chance?"

Mary's flip-flopping heart had landed back in her chest by the time they'd driven the three blocks to Kelley's. The rain was easing up, but her fascination with Jake grew greater with every passing moment.

Of course, she would give them a chance to get better acquainted. He didn't even need to ask. Otherwise, how would she ever know for sure if he was *the one* or not?

After he was introduced to all her crazy family and friends, she would find out if he still wanted to stick around. Or...if by then he was ready to run away—either laughing himself sick or screaming in terror. It would be a good test.

Unbuckling her seat belt, she watched him closely. She was having some trouble believing he was for real. The moment she'd spotted him outside the library, she'd begun pinching herself to be sure she wasn't dreaming. He was almost too good to be true.

After they climbed out of his SUV and headed toward the restaurant's front door, Mary's sister Lucy appeared on her way out. Lucy's arms were loaded down with take-out food packages.

Mary gave Lucy a peck on the cheek. "Jake Pierson, I want you to meet my sister Lucy Walsh."

"Hey, good to meet Mary's sister. Need some help carrying those things?" Jake opened his arms and grinned like a Boy Scout.

"I guess so...Jake, was it?" Lucy gave her sister a raised-eyebrow look, as if to say, *Where'd you hook this one?*

Jake took the packages and then waited for Lucy to show the way to her car. Lucy didn't seem to be in any hurry to leave now that her arms were free, and Mary couldn't figure out how to give her sister the hint.

"I was sorry to hear about your father," Jake told her. "It must be hard having to wonder where he'd been all those years."

Lucy nodded sharply at Jake but turned to Mary without making a reply. "You're not coming to quilting club tonight? We haven't seen you in a while."

"That group is a bunch of gossips," Mary complained—before she realized that Jake was listening closely. "I'm in the process of changing my life, Lucy. Quilting doesn't fit the image in my head of the new me."

Mary turned to Jake and nearly batted her eyelashes at him before she could catch herself. "My sister owns the knitting store in town." And Mary had been a little jealous of her pretty older sister ever since they'd been in their teens.

She held her breath and waited for Lucy or Jake to make a comment. If Jake liked Lucy more, it might kill her.

Immediately Mary felt guilty. Lucy's life had been no better than Mary's, despite the fact that Lucy looked like every man's fantasy of the girl next door.

Mary understood what her sister had been through. What they'd both been through. No one else on earth had any idea but the two of them. At one time Mary had thought that would keep them close, but now she knew better. Lucy wasn't too crazy about hanging around the one person who shared all her secrets.

In addition to that, Lucy was already engaged to be married. Mary was truly happy for her sister. Truly.

Lucy turned to Jake. "Are you visiting someone in Honey Creek?"

Jake's bright eyes blazed at Lucy as he shifted to the other foot. "I'm in the process of moving to town for business. Just leased a house, in fact. Big old place out in the country."

Mary perked up at the idea of him settling into Honey Creek. "Which house?"

Turning to gaze at her with a look that made her itchy, Jake said, "It's south of town, where Main Street runs under the highway. The agent told me it's known as the old Jenkins place."

"Oh, I've always loved that house," Mary told him. And meant it. "But it's huge. Do you need all that space?"

Jake took his sweet time in giving her an answer and it made her wonder what he had in mind. "Maybe." He twisted back to talk to Lucy. "I'm in commercial real estate and I need an office at home. And I have a...uh... hobby or two. Plus, that place was the only available property anywhere nearby."

Lucy threw him a look, using her patented saccharin grin and all those sparkling white teeth. Mary felt her sister's grin in the pit of her stomach. "We won't keep you, Lucy."

"Mary, can I speak to you...um...in private for a minute?"

"I'll just put these bags in your car if you'll point me in the right direction and give me the key." Jake was smiling like a blue-eyed, broad-shouldered Boy Scout again.

And making Mary wish they could be somewhere— anywhere else—alone.

"Sure. Thanks." Lucy handed him her key and indicated her ancient truck parked at the far end of the lot. "Put them in the front, please."

When Jake was out of earshot, Lucy dragged her sister away from the restaurant's door and off to the side. "Where did you ever find him?"

"We ran into each other in Bozeman. Stunning, isn't he?"

Lucy looked as though she would like to say something else, but checked over her shoulder instead. "Mom tells me you're thinking of taking time off from work this week. Is that true?"

"Uh...yeah." This wasn't what Mary thought her sister wanted to talk about. Confused, she went along. "Why?"

Lucy lowered her voice. "Would you do me a huge favor, sis? I can't do it myself. I can't leave the shop during the day. And besides…if I did this, everyone in town would start gossiping about me again."

"Tell me what you need. I'll try."

"Go see Damien Colton." Lucy twisted her head, looking behind them. "See if he's okay and if he needs anything. Please?"

"All the way over to Montana State Prison?" The idea of entering a place with hundreds of male prisoners made Mary sweat with apprehension. "That's a hundred miles away. Why can't you simply wait until he gets out and comes home? That shouldn't take too much longer, should it?"

Lucy took her hand and Mary felt her sister trembling. "I can't speak to Damien directly. You know people will talk. As it is, they either think I hate Damien or secretly still love him. I wouldn't want Steve finding out."

"Your fiancé has to know what happened back then. Why would it…?"

"Mary, please. I don't want to talk to Damien in person. I don't want to plant any ideas in his head about me still caring for him."

"But you want me to ride all the way over there by myself to check on him?" Mary shook her head. "Don't you think he might get the wrong idea about that?"

Tears leaked from the corners of Lucy's eyes. "Can't you just do this one thing for me without making a big deal? I feel terribly guilty about him being in that prison all these years. If it hadn't been for me…"

"Okay, okay, take it easy." Mary felt cornered, as she always did around Lucy. "I'll go."

Lucy threw her arms around Mary and hugged her as though she might not ever have another chance. "Thanks, sis. You're the best."

Jake walked back to the two of them. "You're all set, Lucy."

Thanking him and thanking Mary again, Lucy took back her keys and finally left.

Jake slid his arm around Mary's waist. "What was that all about?"

"Nothing much." But Mary couldn't help thinking of her sister.

Mark Walsh had wreaked havoc on both his daughter's lives, but Mary was determined to take control of her own life. What about Lucy? Could her sister have taken things into her own hands—and killed their father for revenge?

Jake took her hand and walked them toward the front door. "You sure she wasn't concerned about you and me?"

"We didn't talk about you." Not much. But that gave Mary an idea. "I agreed to do Lucy a favor and I'm hoping you'll be willing to help out, too."

"Maybe. What did Lucy need?"

Sighing, Mary would've liked some way to get out of telling him the whole truth, but now she had no choice. "It's a long story. Can we talk about it over supper?"

"Sure." Jake bent to kiss her cheek as he pulled on the front-door handle. "I'm starving."

The touch of his lips sent an immediate and staggering jolt down Mary's spine. She was hungry, too. But not for food.

Chapter 5

Jake leaned back in his chair after the waitress took their orders. He looked around at the many empty tables. He'd eaten here a time or two before as there weren't many restaurants located in the town of Honey Creek. Tonight he'd hoped Kelley's would be packed with locals.

At the moment, though, only a few patrons were at the bar and just two other tables had customers seated for dinner. Something didn't feel right here. The hair on his arms stood straight up. Was someone watching? Who? When he casually glanced up again, pretending to look for their waitress, he couldn't spot anyone or any reason for this odd feeling.

He shook it off as another tangible sign of his guilt. Paranoia. Typical of covert agents. In this case, apparently he and Mary had arrived early for the dinner hour. Disappointed about not having access to lots of Mary's friends, but not ready to give up, Jake decided to take his time and see what information he could obtain while they ate.

"Your sister's a beautiful woman," he began casually. "I'm not sure I would've pegged you two as related though."

Mary's eyes narrowed at him. "Yes, she's always been the pretty one."

That was *not* what he'd meant. "If anyone ever said such a thing, they were wrong." He found himself reaching across the table for her hands. "You are infinitely better-looking than Lucy."

On top of that, Lucy was still someone he suspected in the murder of her father. If Mark Walsh's murder was a crime of passion instead of being connected to an international money-laundering scheme, Lucy could well have done the crime. Something in her eyes screamed *secrets*.

Mary was still staring at him but her gaze had softened. Amber points of light in her eyes danced in the low illumination coming from a wall sconce above her head. In his opinion, she was most definitely the prettier of the two sisters.

Gorgeous. With long, silky red hair lying seductively against her back. With her lush full breasts tempting him as they pushed against the material of her dress. And with her perfectly rounded hips and those erotic thighs—hiding now from his view.

Jake closed his eyes for a second and wished to hell he had never seen her naked.

"I have to explain what took place fifteen years ago so you'll understand why Lucy wants my help." Mary took a sip of water and looked around the room before she continued. "You need to know Lucy's story. And the truth about my father." She made a face with that remark as if she'd suddenly remembered that what had happened fifteen years ago was all her father's fault.

"But mostly it's the story of a man named Damien Colton, who was very young at that time. Barely twenty."

Jake nodded. "Is he related to the sheriff, Wes Colton?"

"Yes. His brother." Mary lowered her voice to a whisper and he had to lean in to hear her words.

"If this is too hard for you..." Jake reached over and touched her arm. He needed to keep her talking. Making her believe that he didn't care one way or the other whether she continued was one excellent method of manipulating her into doing the opposite.

Part of the covert agent's training manual.

Mary shook her head. "You have to hear this. If not from me, then someone else will tell you. You see, my father was a difficult man to live with." Hesitating, she put her fingers to her mouth. "Sorry, I guess I already mentioned that. But back to my sister. She was sixteen then and thought she was madly in love with Damien, a kid whose family still today owns a huge ranch with lots of acreage near Honey Creek."

Mary's eyes took on a hazy cast as she seemed lost in the past. "My father threatened to run Damien out of town if he didn't leave my sister alone."

"He didn't want her dating a rich kid?"

Mary's eyes came back to focus on him. "My family is fairly well off, about as rich as the Coltons. But that isn't the point. I think my father didn't like the idea of

Lucy dating someone four years older. Damien was a good kid, but I guess he looked a little too rough around the edges."

Jake knew Mary and Lucy came from first-generation family wealth. It was one of the things that had put him off about pretending a relationship with Mary before they'd met. And he had already read this whole story while digging into the FBI files on Mark Walsh. But he needed to encourage Mary to get it all out. Maybe he would learn something new.

"What happened?" he asked casually, taking a sip of water.

"My father's body was found…or at least everyone thought it was his body. And Damien was accused of killing him because my father had threatened him."

"Pretty slim motive."

"I agree." Mary picked up her water glass, too, but only stared at it as though she could see back to that time long ago. "They tried and convicted Damien despite the lack of evidence. Sentenced him to a life prison term for a murder he obviously didn't commit."

"At the time you didn't believe he'd done it?"

Mary shook her head and set the water glass down without drinking. "But most people did."

"Including Lucy?"

"She seemed bitter and angry back then. I thought it was over Damien. But now, I'm not so sure." Mary absently began rubbing her hands together. A sure sign of distress.

"What's the favor Lucy wants?" Jake wanted her to come fully back to the present. To stay with him.

Mary's nose turned up and her mouth twisted as if she'd just tasted something sour. "She wants me to drive over to the Montana State Prison and see Damien. So far no release date has been set and she wants to find out if he needs anything."

Jake could easily guess the truth. "She wants *you* to tell him she's sorry for what happened?"

Mary looked toward him and took a deep breath. "I suppose that's what she wants, yes."

"And you don't want to go?"

"Not alone. That's quite a drive. And…and…"

"I'll go with you." He took her hand again and gazed into her troubled eyes. "If you're planning to do this favor for your sister, just tell me when and I'll make time to go with you."

A meeting with the prisoner might mean a breakthrough in his case. Talking to Damien Colton could bring fresh leads.

"Thank you. Oh, thank you, Jake. I can't tell you how much I appreciate it." Mary released a big breath, as though she'd been holding it awaiting his decision.

Jake would never let her make the trip to the prison alone. He couldn't. She seemed to be dreading it, and he couldn't stand seeing her in anguish.

It wasn't that he thought of her as fragile. He didn't. And she wasn't one of those needy, clingy women who annoyed him. Mary was definitely one of a kind: strong and soft at the same time.

Sensual? Oh, yeah. Intelligent? Definitely. But he couldn't quite put his finger on why he thought she was special. As he considered all her good qualities, his conscience broke in and kicked him in the butt once more for using her the way he had. The way he continued to do.

Then the waitress arrived with armloads of food, giving Jake the perfect excuse to bury his guilt—yet again.

Mary finished her grilled chicken salad slowly. She even left some of it untouched on the plate. Both those actions, eating slowly and leaving part of the food behind, were things she had never done in her previous life. But she now knew both would help keep the weight off.

Being with Jake was apparently going a long way toward turning her life around. She still had a craving for the gooey chocolate cake that was a favorite at Kelley's Cookhouse, but she ordered coffee along with Jake instead of dessert.

Proud of herself, she relaxed back in her chair and watched him. The man had no idea how sensual, passionate and exciting he was. Something deep inside her yearned for him. It was more than the sex—though she thought that part had been great. Better than great— for a first time. And she suspected it would only become more intense with practice.

She'd always had a knack for picking up nuances and hints from people, and Jake gave off terrific vibes. Well, okay, he obviously had a few secrets that he hadn't shared. Didn't everyone?

But he was clearly a good man. An honest man. Her heart fluttered, actually fluttered, when he caught her watching him and grinned.

"You've always lived in Honey Creek?" he asked.

"My whole life except for a couple of years at college. It's my home."

"That must be nice. I don't have any place I can really call a home."

She wanted to tell him that he could make a home right here—with her. But she knew it was too early in their relationship to talk about a future. They still didn't know enough about each other, despite the fact that they'd seen each other naked.

The idea of them naked made her blush. She dropped her gaze to the tabletop, letting her hair cover her face so he couldn't see her embarrassment. Why had she insisted on them making love on the very first night they'd met? It had been risky, but she didn't regret it for one second. Even if it meant they could never get past that one night and form a real relationship.

"What are you thinking about?" he asked gently. "You're too quiet."

"I was just wondering if you had any brothers or sisters. Is your mother still alive? Where is your father?"

"Whoa. Lots of questions there." He took a last sip of coffee and studied her from across the table for a moment. "My mother died when I was about ten. No brothers or sisters—that I know of. And I have no idea whether my father is alive or dead. When I finally broke free of his influence, I never looked back."

Mary understood immediately. Jake didn't have anyone or anyplace to call his.

When she didn't make any comments about what he'd told her, he asked his own question. "I know about your father's death, and I've met your sister Lucy, but what about other sisters and brothers? What about your mother?"

"My mom is going strong." As Mary thought about

her mother, it made her warm and smiley all over. "She lives on the hobby farm where I grew up—where I still live. Right north of town. And she runs the family businesses that my father left her. With a lot of help from her boyfriend, that is."

"Your mother has a boyfriend?"

That idea made her smile, too. "Craig Warner. An extremely nice man. I couldn't have picked a better guy for my mom. He was my father's accountant for years before he became CFO of the family's company."

"Craig knew your father?"

"Sure. They were in business together before my father faked his own death." The nasty memory of her father's betrayal brought another thought into her mind. "I can't help wondering where my father really was all those years. Isn't it curious?"

Jake's eyes turned steely gray. Instead of answering, he asked a question of his own. "Do you think Craig Warner knew where your father was? I mean, maybe he did, considering they were partners."

"No way." That was one question she didn't need to ask. "Craig would never have done that to my mother. Or to us kids. You can't imagine how difficult life was for all of us after my father's...uh...first murder. Craig helped us through it."

Jake put his hands out, palms down, as though he was trying to gentle a horse. "I didn't mean anything by asking. I only wanted to know what goes into making you who you are. How you think. That's all."

Mary realized her back had straightened impossibly and her shoulders were high and tight. She shook them down and sat back in the chair, taking a last sip of cool coffee to hide her nerves behind the oversize mug.

"Do you have other brothers and sisters?" Jake leaned on his elbows and tilted his head to watch her. "You said 'us kids.' How many are there?"

"There's four of us. Two boys and two girls. Me and Lucy. And our brothers Peter and Jared."

Jake nodded and gave her a wicked grin. "Exactly the right size of family. Do all of you live in Honey Creek? Still on the family farm?"

Mary felt the flush creeping up her neck again, but she fought it down. "I'm the only one still at home." Yeah, and at twenty-nine wasn't that extremely attractive?

She raced to shine a light on a different subject. "Right now Lucy is living above her store—until she and her fiancé get married. And my brothers have both been gone from home a long time.

"Peter is a single dad and lives with his son in a nice house near downtown." Mary kept talking, desperate to use anything to keep the conversation off herself. "My baby brother Jared is far away—getting started in a finance career. I'm not exactly sure where he's living at the moment. He was in New York, but I think he's been taking special training at his company's Washington, D.C., home office for the past few months."

Jake knew a lot about Jared—probably more than Mary knew. But he was under orders not to reveal anything about the youngest Walsh brother.

Instead he refocused the conversation on the other brother. "What does Peter do for a living?"

Mary's whole face dimpled. "My brother is a private investigator. He has a terrific business, but mostly he works outside of Honey Creek. Not much going on around here for him to investigate. This town is what you might call quiet."

Jake almost laughed, but kept his face in a neutral position. Honey Creek was absolutely seething with crime and suppressed passions. The place was anything but quiet.

Her brother, Peter Walsh, had not been involved in the murder. No motive and no opportunity. But the idea of Mary's mother, Jolene, having a romantic relationship with her dead husband's partner had tweaked Jake's lawman's antenna.

Something for him to consider. To pick apart and inspect for hidden motives. In fact, Jake needed to wrangle an introduction to both Jolene and Craig Warner real soon.

Reaching out, he took Mary's hand across the table again and winked at her. He had to swallow back the bubbling guilt, an emotion that was becoming a constant irritant. But while ignoring it and everything else churning in his gut, he leaned in for a quick kiss. After all, what could be wrong with wanting to meet his new girlfriend's family?

It took a couple of days to arrange their visit with Damien in prison, but they were finally on their way. Jake had taken care of the details. Meanwhile, Mary spent most of that time sweeping up her old life and packing it away in boxes.

At one point yesterday her mother saw her leaving the house carrying her *fat* clothes to the car for donation. "What's going on with you?" her mother had asked. "First the vacation from work and now cleaning out your closets. If I didn't know better, I would say you were in love. Is this about that new man in town Lucy says she met?"

Mary murmured something under her breath to indicate her life was on a new track. She wasn't quite ready to tell her mother how she felt about Jake—since Mary barely knew her own feelings on the subject.

Glancing over at Jake now in the driver's seat, she couldn't help wondering why, after over a week, they'd yet to have a repeat performance of their first night. Sure, he'd given her a peck on the cheek a few times. And once or twice he'd surprised her with a deep, warm kiss. But all their encounters were short-lived and fairly chaste. No secret touches. No glassy-eyed looks that promised remarkable things to come.

Mary couldn't quite put it all together in her mind. But then, maybe all newbies felt as lost at first as she did. She wished this was something she could comfortably ask her mother. Or talk over with her BFF Susan. But she couldn't. Talking would mean actually admitting that she'd been twenty-nine before her first sexual encounter.

Every time she thought of it in those terms the whole thing sounded more and more outrageous.

"You're awfully quiet again this afternoon." Jake glanced over at her and opened his hands on the steering wheel. "Have I done something wrong?"

"Not at all. You've been perfect." Too damned perfect. What the hell was wrong with him? "I was just thinking."

"Thinking about what?"

"How pretty it is in this part of the state."

Ever since they'd passed through Butte, traveling on Interstate 90, the mountains had gotten higher and the trees more lush. As she looked out the windshield now, she spotted Elk Park Pass on their right and Mount

Haggin to the left. They'd been dropping down into a wide valley ripe with bunch-grass prairie.

"See the silky lupine and those blanket flowers? Aren't they colorful?"

"All I see are miles and miles of cattle and fences. What are you talking about?"

"Purple and yellow wildflowers. Beautiful this time of year. The mountains off in the distance always look like a picture postcard during August, too."

Jake grinned as he looked out the window. "If you like the mountains in August, maybe we should take Highway 12 over the pass on the way back. It's a little out of the way, but this is a terrific time of year for sightseeing. What do you think?"

"Maybe."

A highway sign announcing their imminent approach to Deer Lodge and to the prison sent a sudden chill down Mary's spine even in the bright sunshine of the warm day. The idea of prisoners—of a prison with no escape—landed heavily in Mary's gut.

That does it. You know where fat, ugly little girls belong. Go! Echoes of curses spoken long ago rang in Mary's head. *No. No. Please don't lock me in there.*

Mary covered her face and breathed in and out of her mouth trying to slow her speeding pulse.

"What's wrong? Are you okay?"

"I'm…" She lifted her head and tried to find somewhere else to focus her attention—anywhere instead of the looming prison.

"I'm fine. Maybe a little tired of riding." She stared out her window and gazed into the outside rearview mirror, desperate for something else to see—to say.

"Hey, they're not back there anymore," she said

without thinking. "I figured for sure they must be going to the prison, too."

"Huh? Who's not where?" Jake checked his mirror and then glanced over to her with the question in his eyes.

"Oh, nobody, I guess. It's just that I noticed a fancy four-wheel-drive truck following us out of Honey Creek, and I've seen them behind us several times since."

Jake suddenly pulled his SUV off to the side of the Interstate and put his foot on the brake. "What did the truck look like exactly?" His eyes were tight. His mouth a narrow line.

"Jeez, Jake, I don't know. It was black. Big. Shiny. With loads of chrome. I've never seen it before around town."

He started up the SUV again and pulled back on the highway. "If you ever see that truck again...or any vehicle that seems to be following us, I want to know right away. Understand?"

Wow. What the heck was that all about?

Chapter 6

Jake stood behind Mary's chair with his arms folded over his chest and his mind racing behind what he hoped was a stoic expression. She'd been acting as if coming to this prison was a death sentence.

He'd asked her twice if something was going on. But she wouldn't discuss it. Only said she was a little tired and nervous about seeing Damien.

Whatever was affecting her head, he must've caught it, too. He couldn't imagine what was wrong with him that he hadn't noticed a truck following them. In ten years of undercover work, he had never been this sloppy.

"You have twenty minutes." The guard ushered Damien into the visitors' room and left to stand at the door.

Jake paid close attention to Mary's expression and

body movements. He'd figured she'd been lying about something having to do with Damien and that was why she'd been jumpy. But as the prisoner sat down across from her, she never flinched and actually smiled at the guy.

"Do you remember me, Damien?"

The prisoner was big—and threatening—at around six foot four. His dark brown shaggy hair hung down around his collar. He had muscles on top of muscles. No question they came from prison workouts. Physical training was a typical way for prisoners to pass their long days.

"The guard told me Mary Walsh was here to see me," Damien said with a sneer. "But if he hadn't told me I wouldn't have known. You look different, kid. You've turned into a real babe."

Jake fisted his hands at his sides and fought the urge to force those words back down Damien Colton's throat. Prison hadn't done much for this jerk's attitude. Whatever he might have been at twenty had obviously been beaten out of him in here. Now he was nothing more than an ordinary head-up-his-ass con.

"I... Thanks," Mary told the bastard. "My friend Jake came with me." She waved her hand toward him standing behind her. "Lucy asked me to come."

"Why?" The bitterness suddenly rolled off Damien like sheets of rain. "Why now? I haven't heard one word from her in fifteen long years. Lucy couldn't even be bothered to come to my trial. And after fifteen years she has something to say now? Now, when I'm finally done with this hell and about to be released?"

Damien spewed out a string of curses, making Jake wonder if Mary should still be sitting there listening to him vent his anger. This wasn't even her fight. She was only the messenger.

Jake took a step closer to Mary, but she spoke up before he reached her. "I agree with you, Damien. Lucy tends to think of only herself. But it's not one hundred percent her fault. You remember what she went through?"

"Bull." Damien pounded his fist on the table. "She went through nothing compared to what I went through with that bastard. Whatever Lucy wants from me at this point, tell her it's too damned late."

"She's engaged to be married, Damien. I'm sure she doesn't want anything from you. Finding out that our father was actually alive all those years has been a big shock for us. I think…I think she just wants you to know she's sorry."

Jake watched defeat pour into Damien's eyes. "Yeah? Well, her sorry can't even buy me an extra minute of freedom. Tell her I don't need it, and I sure as hell don't want it."

Mary sighed and rose from her chair. "I'll tell her. Is there anything else I can do for you? Any other messages you want me to take back to Honey Creek before you get out?"

Damien hung his head as though he was ashamed of his behavior toward Mary, a woman who had never harmed him and had always believed in his innocence. "No. I'll carry my own messages."

Mary grimaced and sighed again. "Okay. Bye, Damien."

Before she could turn away, Damien said, "You shouldn't have come, Mary. I'm…sorry."

The corners of her mouth turned up in a weak version of a smile. "Goodbye." She turned and left the room.

Jake stood where he was for another second. "Are you planning on coming back to Honey Creek?"

Damien looked up at him from where he remained seated. "You're some kind of cop, aren't you?"

Crap. "No. I'm in real estate."

"Liar. I've spent the bulk of my adult life learning to spot narcs. What do you want from me?"

Jake looked Damien straight in the eyes. "I came here for Mary. She's fiercely loyal to her sister, so she came all the way out here for her—and for you. She cares about you as an old friend, Colton."

The prisoner stared at him with absolute misery in his eyes. Jake's few words didn't seem like enough of an explanation.

"Give Mary time," Jake added. "She'll come around and accept your apology."

Jake took one of the biggest risks of his entire covert career and pulled a blank card from his pocket. "When you get out, if there's anything you want to…say. Or anything you need help with, call this number."

He scribbled down the FBI field office number on the back of the card and laid it on the table. Jake wondered if he wasn't coming out of cover to one of the bad guys. But his gut told him that Damien Colton was not the murdering type. He didn't even seem like the criminal type. Not to mention, this Colton was probably too young when he went to prison to be involved in any money-laundering schemes.

Turning his back, Jake sent up a quiet prayer for

the man's soul. Damien had been wronged. Terribly wronged. And he might never be able to recover from it.

Damien fingered the card for the tenth time as he waited for his phone call to go through. He'd almost torn the thing up twice, but something had made him hold on to it. Finally, he'd stuck the paper card down into his shoe, deciding to tear it up later. He looked around to find out if anyone was watching.

Seeing no one, he breathed deeply just as his call was answered. "Hello, Darius?"

"Ah. The black sheep calls. What do you want from me, Damien?" Darius Colton sounded as distant and cold as ever.

Damien bit his tongue to keep from begging his father for help. "My court-appointed attorney isn't returning my phone calls. I want to know why it's taking so long to clear up the paper work for my release."

"Not my problem, son. I told you fifteen years ago that I'd spent my last penny on your defense."

Yes, Damien remembered it distinctly. As devastating as being convicted of murder had been, learning that a few family members believed in his guilt was enough to drive any remaining love for them away for good.

"But now that you know I'm innocent can't you at least make a phone call or two?"

Darius Colton mumbled something under his breath. Then he said, "The system will let you out of prison eventually. Wait your turn. No one remembers or cares about you anymore."

"That's not true, Dad. People do remember me. Mary Walsh came to see me today."

"The librarian? Mark Walsh's fat kid? I don't believe she came all that way by herself."

Damien blew out another breath and counted to five. "She's not fat now. And she came with a friend. Not anyone I remember from Honey Creek."

"Sure she did. Who?"

The question was abrupt and it took Damien aback. This was getting him nowhere. He should never have contacted his father for help.

"Just skip it," he said. "I'll wait. Don't…"

"I'll contact your brother Wes." Darius's interruption was another shock. "Maybe the sheriff can do something to speed things along. But that's the best I can do."

"Sure," Damien said as he let the sarcasm drip from his words. "Wouldn't want to put you out."

"What are your plans for after the release?"

Damien couldn't help himself, the opportunity to dig at his father was too good to pass up. "Thought I would come back and live off you, Dad. The Colton ranch can be a good life."

Actually, ranch life was exactly what Damien had in mind for his future. Not the Colton ranch, of course. But it would have to be a jumping-off point. He needed time to get his feet on the ground.

Darius was quiet for a long moment until at last he said, "Your mother wants you back on the ranch. You can come home—for a while. But I'll expect you to work while you're here."

Sighing, Damien gave up. He had never been able to figure his father out beyond his womanizing and secretive business deals. And it didn't sound as if fifteen years had done anything to make the man more transparent.

"Right, Darius. Well, I guess I'll see you when I see you then."

Hanging up and cursing his father under his breath, Damien swore to put all of Honey Creek in his rearview mirror as soon as possible.

"If you don't still want to do this, we can turn around and head back to Honey Creek the more direct way." Mary looked over at Jake's profile and could see his jaw twitching.

"I promised you the ride," he muttered. "And it will work out fine. It's only that it's getting late. I'm afraid your pretty views will turn to darkness before we reach the top of the mountains. Not much sightseeing to do after dark."

As their SUV put distance between them and the state prison, Mary felt herself relaxing more and more. She'd done it. Walked in and out of a prison with her head held high and with hardly any discernable shaking at all. Now she could breathe easy and enjoy the rest of the day.

Not so for Jake. With each passing mile, he seemed to become more tense. He kept checking the rearview mirror and shifting in his seat.

She decided to turn the tables on him. "You're the one that's quiet now. What are you thinking about?"

Maybe he was disappointed in her. Mary had so hoped he would trust her to know what she was doing. She couldn't bear to explain why it had been so important for her to see Damien and to help her sister. But she wasn't sorry they'd come.

"Seeing Colton back there reminded me that your father was recently murdered." Jake didn't take his eyes off the road ahead as they began their ascent up the grade. "Have you given any thought to who might've wanted him dead?"

The idea was laughable, but she chose not to admit it by frowning. "I would imagine there might be tens of people out there in the world—maybe hundreds of people—who could've killed him. At the risk of repeating myself..."

Jake did the laughing for her, but he didn't sound amused. "Yeah, I know. *He was a difficult man.* But seriously, you must have thought about it."

She wasn't going to talk to him about the members of her family and their many reasons to want Mark Walsh dead. Instead she began with the rest of the community.

"My father's name was linked with several women. Women who might've had hot-tempered boyfriends or could've been a little unbalanced themselves. Any one of them would've been happy to see my father dead."

"You think it was a crime of passion?"

"Sure. What else?"

Jake shrugged and shook his head. "How about business associates? I hear your father first got rich in the liquor trade. The Walsh breweries are legendary. That's not an easy business. Brewing is rumored to have mob connections. Maybe he stepped on toes and paid for it."

Mary was pleased she and Jake were talking over the past—sort of. She liked that he cared and was curious. But she wasn't entirely sure that digging up the past was a smart thing to do.

Deciding to go with being happy about his attention, she said, "My father had a lot of help in the early days of the business. My mother and Craig did most of the real work putting that business on the map. And there's a story that Darius Colton, Damien's dad, lent my father some money just when he needed it the most. I simply can't believe that the mob would do business with my dad. He was…"

"Difficult." Jake's chuckle was for real this time. He glanced over at her and winked. "I know. But I think it's interesting to sort through all the suspects who might've done the crime. Like a murder mystery."

Mary laughed out loud. "Well, it would be a lot more fun if it wasn't my father we were talking about. But yes, we could do that. You'd need to meet the people involved, though. Maybe you could come to one of my mother's famous barbecues. Would you like that?"

Jake reached over and touched her hand. "Sounds good. I want to meet your friends. But don't you think we should check with your mother?"

"Sure, but Mom…" Mary stopped talking and gasped. "Oh, look at that."

They'd rounded a hairpin turn and caught the tail end of a spectacular sunset. Jake pulled the SUV out onto a lookout point and put the transmission in Park, idling the engine and watching the sun going down through the windshield.

This was why she'd wanted to come the long way. This sight. Even though the sun was setting behind their backs, the road they were traveling had enough twists and turns to afford terrific views of both the mountains and the sky.

Streaks of copper, peppered with raspberry points, spread out to the indigo heavens from a cheddar-colored base of sun. Beautiful sunsets never lasted long in the mountains. But as this one eased over the bumpy horizon, it shimmered with colors reminiscent of the best rainbow she'd ever seen.

Mary sighed. "This trip was definitely worth the extra time. Thank you, Jake."

When she looked toward him, he was already watching her.

"Definitely worth it." He leaned in and surprised her with a sensual kiss. Warm and tender, but also full of longing and promise.

As he pulled away and sat back, he whispered, "You are every bit as beautiful as that sunset, Mary. Damned straight it was worth the…"

Mary felt the jolt before she heard the screech of tires. "Jake!" Someone had hit them from behind—hard.

"I'm on it! Hang on."

The SUV roared to life as Jake threw it into gear and took off. He stepped on the gas and sped around the rest of the curve, barreling toward the crest of the mountain.

"What are you doing? You can't leave the scene of an accident. What if someone was hurt?"

"That was no accident. Tighten your seat belt."

What? Not an accident? Then that had to mean someone deliberately ran into them. But why?

As she tugged at her seat belt, Mary looked into the side mirror but saw nothing. Nothing but the blackness of after-dusk in the mountains. Turning to Jake, she started to question what he'd said.

But before she could open her mouth, he thundered out another order. "Brace yourself. They're closing in."

She didn't need to flick another glance in the mirror

to notice bright headlights suddenly close behind them. Too close.

And too bright. The whole inside of their SUV lit up like a sunshine-filled morning.

"Jake!"

He didn't answer as he fought the wheel and stepped down harder on the gas. In the glare of their own headlights, Mary could see one more hairpin turn coming up ahead. If they got hit from behind there, it was a five-hundred-foot drop over the side.

Mary held her breath while Jake urged the SUV to go faster down the hill toward the turn. She noticed the headlights behind them growing slightly dimmer as they raced on in the dark. No one could take these turns at high speeds. It was insane.

But Jake never slowed as he entered the next turn. Mary closed her eyes and put her hands over her mouth to keep from screaming. She heard the brakes, felt the tires skidding sideways and waited for the worst.

Next, her body righted and she noticed the SUV was coming out of its skid. Suddenly it took what felt like a quick ninety-degree right turn. Into the mountain side?

Then they stopped. The engine quit roaring and began to purr.

Mary's eyes popped open, but everything around her was black. Their headlights and dashboard lights were off. She glanced in Jake's direction and opened her mouth to ask what had happened. All she could manage was one squeak.

"Shush," he whispered. "One more moment and..."

From behind them she heard another engine whining and brakes squealing. She shifted all the way around in her seat and looked out the back. As she watched, a big truck flew by on the highway about twenty feet behind their SUV.

Realizing she was still holding her breath, she exhaled and said, "Do you think they spotted us?"

"Hope not. But they'll figure it out when they hit a flat stretch a few miles ahead."

"Where are we?"

"According to the GPS, on a fire road. Good thing I noticed it coming up."

"Does the fire road go anywhere?"

Jake took in a gulp of air, as if to calm himself, and checked his screen. "It meanders around through the highest peaks and eventually comes out on the Interstate right north of Butte. Or at least it's supposed to. I'm not crazy about driving it in the dark, but I don't think we've got a lot of choices."

She sat back in her seat and fought the tears. "You saved us. Where did you learn how to drive like that?"

Turning the headlights back on, Jake put the SUV in gear and eased on the gas. "One of my many hobbies. I once took a defensive driving course."

Mary found it hard to believe anyone could learn how to do what he'd done in driving school. But she wasn't going to question her good fortune at having Jake at the wheel.

There were other questions running through her shaky brain, however. "Why did they come after us? Why would anybody want to hurt us?"

Through the dim light, glowing off dashboard, she saw Jake grinding his teeth.

It took him a moment or two more to answer. "I have

no idea. I would hope it doesn't have anything to do with our seeing Damien Colton in prison."

"No way. Couldn't be." But the next thing to occur to Mary's mind was a far less logical supposition. "Do you think it might be connected to my father's murder?"

"I hope not." Jake cleared his throat and concentrated his gaze straight ahead. "But we can talk about it more when we get back to my house."

"Am I going to your house?" Though her whole body was still trembling from their ordeal, the idea of going home with him made her hot.

"Absolutely," Jake told her. "If that truck had hit us a little harder or it had been a more direct hit, we would be at the bottom of a canyon by now. I nearly lost you—and I'm not letting you out of my sight tonight."

Chapter 7

Mary walked in his footsteps with her fingers stuck through his belt loops in the back. She was close enough that Jake could even feel her erratic breathing on his neck.

He stood still for a moment and whispered to her, "What are you doing? Keep a step or two behind me."

"You said to stay close." Her whispered remark sounded jumpy—nervous.

"Not that close." He eased her back a couple of feet.

It was bad enough that he'd had to sweep his rental house for intruders without benefit of a weapon at the ready. But how would he go about explaining a Glock 9 mm to a woman who thought his job was in real estate? He'd left that weapon under the seat of his SUV. And though he'd stashed several other weapons around the house, he wanted to stay undercover—for the time being.

However, Jake couldn't hope to do a thorough security check as long as Mary's body heat kept seeping through his shirt, mixing with his blood and driving him wild.

"This house is huge." Mary apparently changed her mind and found his intruder check boring.

She wandered off into the open-concept kitchen, where he'd left a soft light burning over the range. "Why would you need a professional chef's kitchen?"

"To cook food."

She swung back to look at him as he closed the storage closet door. "You? You cook?"

"Sure. Give me a few minutes to check all the doors and windows and I'll make you a late supper."

Mary went back to opening refrigerator and pantry doors, exclaiming how well-supplied and neat everything was. Meanwhile Jake made sure every downstairs door and window was secure, each one locked up as tight as he'd left it.

Mentally chastising himself, he took the stairs two at a time to secure the second story, leaving Mary to ooh and ahh over the furnishings in the dining room/ kitchen combination. Yes, he had a well-stocked kitchen and expensive decorator furniture, but he hadn't taken the damned time to ask the Bureau to alarm the house. What an idiot. Now he would have to phone in and plead for emergency service to set up a security system ASAP. Turkey that he was.

But this house was just for show. Or rather it had started out that way when he'd begun this mission a few weeks ago. He'd never planned on using it as a safe house. All he did was sleep here once in a while.

At the thought of sleep and beds, he wondered how the sleeping arrangements would go for him and Mary tonight. He didn't want her going back to the Walsh farm—not until he got a better handle on who had attacked them and found help protecting her.

But he had made a vow not to touch her again after their one crazy and erotic night. He'd already listed a hundred reasons in his head why they shouldn't have slept together in the first place—and why they should never do it again.

But making love to her again had become all he could think about. Day and night. It didn't matter whether she was with him for real or if he was only dreaming about her. He was consumed with thoughts of her.

Rolling his eyes at his own ridiculous notions, he thanked heaven this house was big. Lots of bedrooms.

Hmm. But lots of bedrooms might not be enough to keep him out of her bed.

Finishing his security check, Jake headed down the front stairs with his mind racing. How could he arrange things to make it easy for him to keep his hands off her?

Walking through the two-story open family room, Jake had the only idea that made any sense. He would send her upstairs and he would sleep down here in front of the fire.

That should do it.

He hoped. Unless he started walking in his sleep.

"Hi," she said when she spotted him turning on lights. "Everything okay?"

God, he hoped it would be. "The house is secure. Now let's see what we've got for supper."

"You have *everything* in your kitchen. All the

ingredients and utensils for any meal you could possibly want."

"Don't count on that." The only meal he wanted to eat was standing right before him. "I was top chef in a San Francisco restaurant in another life. I have a repertoire of recipes."

"Cool. Then you decide what you want to cook. Me? I'm a top eater."

They both laughed and Jake actually began to relax. This might not be so tough. He only had to get through one night of protecting her alone before he could call in reinforcements.

How hard could that be?

A couple of hours later Jake was finding out exactly how *hard* things could get. He'd fisted his hands to keep from reaching for Mary enough times that his nails had caused permanent damage to the skin on his palms.

"That was a terrific meal." Mary stood to carry her plates to the kitchen.

"Thanks. It's my healthy take on eggs Benedict. The sauce is made from low-fat yogurt, lemon juice and lemon zest instead of the usual hollandaise."

"You're hired," Mary said with a chuckle as she reached the sink. "You can be my personal chef from now on."

Jake didn't figure either his palms or his groin could stand the strain. "Leave the dishes. Let's have coffee and the flan in the family room in the other wing. I think it's chilly enough to light the fire."

"Okay." She turned slowly and brushed past him to move out of his way.

He caught a whiff of her hair—strawberries—and his knees went weak. Standing by the sink, he grabbed hold of the countertop edge with both hands and counted to ten.

This was going to be one hell of a long night.

Minutes later, Jake carried the coffee and dessert in on a silver tray. Mary was kneeling by the hearth, lighting the kindling.

When she saw him, she grinned. "It's odd to think of it being cold enough in August for a fire. But the nights have been particularly chilly this year. Down to the mid-thirties last night. Although they can withstand much cooler, the farmhands covered the chicken coop to keep the birds warm."

"I forgot you live on a farm."

Mary stood and dusted off her hands while the kindling crackled behind her back. "It's not as much of a farm as it used to be. Everyone in my family has a busy life and no time to mess with farming or the animals anymore." She closed one eye and thought about what she was saying. "Well, no one has time except for me. But I've never been involved much with the farm. Not even as a kid. I was always more into books."

Jake set the tray on the coffee table and pulled the table away from the sofa so they could lounge in front of the fire and also reach the cups and plates at the same time. "Come sit down and let's talk more about who had a motive to kill your father."

She plopped down into the overstuffed sofa and sighed. "This is nice. The kindling has caught. We should have a lovely roaring fire soon. You go first."

He poured the coffee. "I don't know any of the people involved—except for you and Lucy. And I don't think either of you would have a motive. You have to start with a suspect and I'll offer my opinion."

She accepted a mug of coffee and looked up at him across the rim. "I don't like thinking about the people I know having a motive for murder."

Jake reached over and touched her cheek. "This is only to pass the time. But if you'd rather not—"

Mary closed her eyes and bit her lip until he stopped stroking her skin. He understood. His own mind had wandered dangerously while the warmth from her flesh moved through his fingers.

"Um." She cleared her throat and tensed her shoulders. "What if whoever killed my father is also trying to kill me? Someone tried to run us off the road, remember."

He could scarcely forget. "Would your father's murderer have reason to kill you, too?"

"No." She shook her head once, then hedged. "I don't know. I don't think so. But they might think I know something or someone that I don't."

When she looked up at him again, her eyes filled with fear. "Oh, Jake. I might be in trouble and not even know why."

He couldn't stand it. Taking the mug from her hand, he put it aside and scooted in close to put his arms around her. Her whole body quivered.

"That's why you're staying with me tonight." His confident remark sounded cocky, but he couldn't help saying whatever it took to make her feel safe. "You'll be okay here."

She must've believed him because in a moment, she slipped off her shoes and sat back. Sighing, she flexed her feet in front of the fire.

Toeing off his own boots, he noted his heartbeat

kicking into overdrive. Beneath Mary's normally calm exterior he'd sensed a constant sizzle of desire whenever they touched—even when passing a dish or exchanging mugs. He could feel a sort of sensual vibration within her that excited and inflamed him.

"Mary…"

She reached over, touching a finger to his lips. "Shush." Stroking each lip, she used her fingertips as though they were her most sensitive body part.

Capturing her hand in both of his, he kissed each finger. Then he turned his attention to the inside of her arm, kissing his way up to the sensitive skin at the elbow and taking a quick nip.

Mary sucked in a breath, jerked and tugged at her arm. But he held her steady.

Smiling, he blew a warm breath against her flesh. "Are you saying you don't want a repeat performance of the other night?"

He hoped to hell she would say no, but his instincts told him her first answer would be yes. As if of its own volition, his hand moved to her waist, and he flattened a palm against her rib cage, letting his knuckles brush the soft underside of her breast.

A corner of her mouth curved up. "I keep forgetting what kind of things we did. Guess I was sort of out of it that night. It might help if you could remind me…"

He brought his mouth down on hers with hungry enthusiasm. As his skin prickled with an erotic flush, he felt the extra blood pounding into his extremities.

Jake couldn't remember when he'd ever met a woman with such a love of life, such honesty, such passion. A woman who laughed heartily, blushed easily and trusted with abandon.

Yet underneath the wide-eyed, trusting librarian he'd glimpsed a strong, decisive woman. Someone he could spend a lifetime getting to know.

Some other lifetime, he reminded himself. After his assignment was over. But after finishing with this life, he would have to move on to the next. And then the next.

Mary squirmed beneath him and his hands were suddenly fondling her ripe breasts. Just where he'd wanted them in the first place.

To hell with the next life. To hell with his assignment. What he wanted—needed—was right here begging him to give and take extraordinary pleasure.

"Make love to me, Jake." Her whisper seemed to hang in the air like heavy perfume.

Claiming her mouth again in a kiss that could be illegal in ten states, he growled his agreement with what she wanted. The sound she made deep in her throat fed his desperation. He tangled his tongue with hers and sucked at her bottom lip.

His lips moved to her jawline as he began kissing his way down her vulnerable neck. Then he discovered his talented fingers had already unbuttoned her blouse and unsnapped her bra. When was the last time he'd used those moves on a woman? He couldn't remember. Too long ago. But all of a sudden he was truly grateful for his body's automatic responses.

As foggy as his mind seemed, he was determined not to have an exact repeat of the other night. This time he would get the bra all the way off.

He urged her arms out of the shirt's sleeves as he kissed his way across her shoulder. "Hello, Ariel," he murmured when the tattoo came under his lips. "Long time no see."

Mary giggled and slipped out of her bra all on her own. Her hands went to his shirt and he suddenly decided they were both too well-dressed for the occasion. Besides, the heat from the fire had become too intense for clothes.

They stripped as he felt droplets of sweat crisscrossing his forehead. Fire fed the hunger, consuming his brain. He took her mouth again and let his hands roam free.

She shuddered and dug her fingers through his hair, arching into his caresses. One last time he desperately tried to fight her effect on him. But it was then he realized his hands had already moved ahead without him. Giving in with no real regret, he replaced his fingers with his mouth, sucking her nipple hard.

"Please, Jake!" Her hands went to his shoulders, frantically trying to hold on while her nails dug into his flesh.

Yes, he would please her again. But this time he had no intention of rushing. He moved to the other breast and her body bowed, the urgent sense of desire rushing through them both. She pressed against him and suddenly he found his erection cradled at the juncture of her thighs.

It took everything in him not to push inside her. To claim her again. Hard and fast. He'd been her first. He wanted to be her only.

Instead of demanding what he wanted, he scooped her up in his arms and carefully placed her on the sofa. He gazed down into her dreamy eyes as she reached out, arms begging for him to come to her.

Going to his knees before her on the soft hearth rug,

he spread her legs and edged between them. He bent his head to steal a quick taste of her lips again. She tasted of coffee and sugar—and of a unique spice that must be one of her own. Running his hands up along the insides of her thighs, he felt her skin quaking under his touch. When his fingers slipped into her wet and warm spot, she went wild.

It took every ounce of his willpower to keep from savaging her. But he was hanging on to sanity by the slenderest of wires.

Moving closer, he rocked his erection against her most tender flesh. Parting her with his fingers, he widened the path for himself.

"Jake!" Her voice was drenched in white heat.

"I like it when you call my name." He slipped inside her and she threw her legs around his waist to hold him in place.

Kissing her forehead, her nose and finally her lips, he gave her gentleness despite what his body desired. He kept his kisses soft, slow and undemanding. When her breathing at last came easier and she opened her lids to look up at him, he found the firelight had jumped into her amber eyes. They were bright with passion.

He started rocking again. Slow. Sure. Her eyes fluttered shut as a sheen of sweat appeared on her skin. He drew her higher, until he heard her breathing turn to labored pants. In that moment he forced himself to stop again, deliberately slowing things down and not taking her too fast—too rough.

She clung to him and gasped for air. He kissed her earlobe, her hair. He wanted her to acknowledge the sensual nature he knew was buried deep within her. For that, he needed her complete trust and realized the only way to get it was to let her set the pace.

If…waiting didn't drive him mad in the meantime.

Mary urged him to begin their sexual dance once more, using a combination of moans and roaming hands. But he gritted his teeth and held on. Then—at last—she began rocking against him.

"Yes," he murmured. He bent to her breast and took one of her nipples into his mouth.

He sucked and she rocked harder. Faster and higher. When he ground his hips against her pushes and then reached between them to flick his thumb across her sensitive nub, she screamed out.

Feeling the pleasure begin to ripple through her, Jake lost all rational thought. He pounded violently, rejoicing as she met him thrust for thrust. In moments, he felt her shudder and let himself go. Driving deep one last time, he saw stars behind his eyelids as they raced over the edge together.

Outside the large country house at that moment, a man named Vanos Papandreou sat in the brush with a pair of infrared glasses trained on the downstairs windows. Known only as the Pro to clients and competitors, he had no trouble waiting for targets to move—even if that meant sitting in a cold drizzle for hours on end. But it appeared that this man and woman were in for the night.

Vanos's orders had come down from his employer. He was not to make any kind of direct assault. No, this client wanted tactics that were only designed to frighten. To scare off a perceived threat from this man. Or failing that, the client wanted every overt move to appear to be an accident.

The Pro's mess-up on the mountain road earlier tonight had only been a slight miscalculation. He'd intended to push the target's SUV off the cliff and then make it look like an unfortunate accident. It had been a perfect setup, too perfect to pass up. Vanos figured he would be due a bonus for quick work. But when his truck didn't hit the SUV squarely, Vanos was surprised at his target's superior driving skills.

His employer had said the target might be in law enforcement. Vanos could now confirm that assessment.

But it didn't matter. Over the years Vanos's targets had ranged from Secret Service agents to a twelve-year-old boy and everywhere in between. The boy had bothered him—for a while—but the money had been excellent on that job, coming from a stepbrother who wanted the kid's inheritance. Those kinds of major payoffs went a long way toward easing a wayward conscience.

Vanos was known as the Pro for good reason. A professional in every sense, he never missed.

The client in this case wanted scare tactics and accidents. And despite the fact that Vanos was a master marksmen who could hit a moving target at over a hundred yards, what the client wanted was what the client received.

Stashing his night glasses and falling back to his newly rented sedan, Vanos began conjuring up various methods to throw a scare into the man. Perhaps the best idea would be to target the woman?

Perhaps. But whatever methods he decided to use,

Vanos figured he would turn this job into a game. To scare instead of kill.

Yes, this one could be fun.

Chapter 8

Mary awoke when sun came streaming through the blinds and hit her in the eyes. They hadn't slept a whole lot last night. After their spectacular lovemaking session on the sofa in front of the fire, she and Jake had climbed the stairs to his bed—and the party had continued.

A silly grin broke out on her face as she thought of how Jake had reached for her again and again all night long. He'd made her feel needed—special. Mary was feeling much more of everything than she had ever felt. She would never forget the night—or Jake.

Stretching like a lazy cat, she reveled in the odd but sweet aches and the overall languorous feeling she was experiencing. If they decided to stay right here in bed for the rest of the day, she wouldn't care. Actually, they could stay here for the rest of the week.

Rolling over, she reached for Jake, ready to snuggle

up for however long he wanted. But his side of the bed was cold and empty.

She sat straight up and looked around to find herself alone in the bedroom. Listening for running water in the shower, she was disappointed to hear nothing but silence.

Where was Jake?

Deciding he must be downstairs fixing breakfast, she grumbled as she forced herself out of the bed and onto her feet. Food wasn't that important. Not anymore. Mary had found something much better to take her mind off eating.

As she headed for the gigantic master bathroom she considered how, despite its imposing look both from the outside and within some of the rooms, Jake's house seemed warm and inviting. Now she could imagine what Jane Eyre must have felt when she'd first come to Thornfield.

As if she belonged. For maybe the first time in her life.

Hugging herself around the waist, Mary grinned like a fool while walking into the bathroom. She wished for the ability to whistle so that the whole world could see how happy she was. But not a chance. Jolene was the whistler in the family.

After turning on the water for her shower, Mary took a moment to glance around the room. Expecting to see a mess, towels on the floor and water everywhere, she was surprised to see that Jake must have straightened up after both of them last night and after himself this morning.

The man was neat, and the most tender and exciting lover imaginable—and he could cook.

Jake was too good to be true. But that thought stopped her cold. Hadn't Jane Eyre also felt the same about Rochester, her true love and the hero of the book?

But Jane Eyre's love story had been rocky and miserable. She'd found out that her hero was secretly married.

Mary stepped under the shower spray, absently mulling over what her gut instincts had been telling her where Jake was concerned. She had so little experience in the man department that she feared being hasty.

She sensed that Jake was good. Deep-down good. Unlike some of the men in her life up to now. But there was *something*...

As if he were two people, Mary decided as she ran the bar of soap along her chest and belly. Yes, the wonderful-lover-and-good-man side to him had certainly captured her heart. She was far enough gone over that part of him that she almost couldn't remember what had been nagging at her subconscious about his other side.

But then it came to her. Most of the time when Jake looked at her, it was with a combination of heat and tenderness. But on occasion she spotted some emotion in his eyes that didn't match either his words or his actions. Wishing she had enough experience to figure out what that emotion was, Mary finished her shower and dried off, still considering it.

She had seen that look somewhere else besides in his eyes, on someone else—a long time ago. But where? Traipsing back through the bedroom and searching for her clothes, Mary kept sifting through her memories. That look—it was familiar. But...

She suddenly remembered. Her big sister Lucy's eyes had carried that exact same look whenever she'd been feeling guilty about something. As a kid, Lucy was always doing one thing or another that she'd ended up regretting in the end. Stealing Mary's toys when they were little. Stealing a boy Mary had her eye on in junior high. Lying to their mother and father about seeing Damien in high school.

Now that Mary thought it over, the expression was definitely guilt. But Mary didn't have a clue what Jake could be feeling guilty about. Hmm. That wasn't totally true. It could be he was feeling a little guilt over being her first lover. But guilt about taking her virginity was nonsense. She'd begged him. Wanted him to be the one.

Mary hoped with all her heart that wasn't his reason for feeling guilt. But *if* it wasn't, the other possibilities seemed scary. What if he was lying to her about not being married?

A shudder ran along her spine as she finished buttoning up her blouse. She hated the idea, but maybe when she returned to work, she should look him up on the Internet despite her earlier reservations about being sneaky.

Just to prove that he was telling the truth, mind you.

Sitting in a rocker on the house's wide veranda, Jake hung up his secure SAT phone and took a sip from his coffee mug. Grateful the coffee was still warm in the chilled morning air, he looked out at the tangle of pines, Douglas firs and shrub brush surrounding the house.

The entire area encompassing the house had been landscaped with native plantings, making the place look like a mountain ski resort. But at the moment he would've preferred a rolling grass lawn where one could easily see out to every inch of ground. A moment ago he'd finished speaking to his partner Jim about the incident on the road last night and was told that a security alarm team would have to be sent from the Denver field office. It could take days, if not a full week, to free up a team.

Jake knew how alarm systems worked and probably would've been able to install a system himself, but he didn't have the necessary equipment. Frustrated, he wondered how long he could go on like this. Undercover life was no kind of life anymore. He felt as if he'd been living in purgatory for the past few years—neither in heaven nor hell. Just living.

Mary came to mind and Jake tried to will away her image. His guilt on her account had become debilitating. His mind would barely focus on the investigation. What good was a covert agent who couldn't keep his head in the game?

Last night with Mary had shaken him. Consumed him. Not only the sex—past his compulsion where Mary was concerned and way beyond the guilt, he'd glimpsed heaven in her bed.

How was he supposed to walk away from that and go back to purgatory? The need to possess her—to be possessed—had transported him right out of the realm of murderers and money-laundering schemes. He had even ignored whatever rules he'd vowed to follow as a covert government agent. Mary dominated him, mind and body, as she'd begged him to take her again and again.

She had given him the biggest gift of his life—hope. Hope that he could actually love another woman. For ten long years, he'd been positive that for him love was only in the past. That Tina had been it for him.

Tina was the love of his life. She'd brought him out of his shell and turned him into a man who could be charming and make friends. She was his partner, his lover, his coach and his most ardent cheerleader.

When she'd died in that car wreck, Jake had thought his life was over. He'd buried himself in his new job as a covert operative—living other people's lives.

Now…now, Mary's sharp intelligence and loving ways had brought him back to life. Back to giving a damn about what he did and whom he hurt.

And what would come of all this life and hope he was feeling? In the end, he would be forced to walk away from her. If for no other reason than that when Mary discovered the truth about his lies, she would never speak to him again. He couldn't blame her, but it would kill him just the same.

"Jake?" Mary stuck her head out of the front door and spied him sitting at the far end of the long veranda. "There you are. I thought I'd lost you."

As she smiled and walked toward him, Jake's heart knew the truth. He loved her—desperately. If all things were equal, he would tell her the truth right now and take his punishment. But things weren't equal in this case. Mary's life was on the line.

He'd already arranged for someone to keep an eye on her when he couldn't. But despite his assignment, he wanted to be the only one who was her protector. No one could do the job the way he could. He would never recover if any disaster befell Mary. With Tina, it had taken years. This time he knew it was worse for him.

Knowing that, he could not. Would not. Let anything happen.

"Breakfast is on the stove," he said as she came close. "You're getting a late start on the morning. What do you have in mind for today?"

Her bottom lip stuck out slightly and it made him chuckle to see her looking petulant. "I would've liked another hour or two in bed—with you."

Standing, he took her into his arms. The kiss he gave her was slow, warm, with a definite promise of things to come. He wanted her to feel what he felt. Wanted to pour out his love through his kiss—his touch. But he knew she needed words. Words he could not give her.

When he let her go and set her back from him, she looked up with glassy eyes. "That's not helping. It only makes me want to go back to bed all the more."

"Ah, but it's going to be a beautiful day." He forced the covert agent inside him to regain control of the situation. "No rain for a change and temperatures will be more like summer. Let's go to town. I want to talk to the sheriff about that attempt on our lives last night."

"It's not Wes's jurisdiction. That cliff was nearly a hundred miles north."

"Yes, I know. But I believe the driver was someone from Honey Creek, don't you? I find it too coincidental that a perfect stranger would want to shove us off the side of a cliff. The assault on us must be connected somehow to your father's murder and the sheriff should know about it."

Mary was shaking her head. "But why? I've thought and thought and I can't come up with a reason why anyone would want me…us dead. It's almost as if someone heard us talking about suspects. But that's not possible."

Jake ran with it. "Maybe it is possible. I don't remember every place where we talked about the murder. We could've accidentally mentioned it in public."

Mary was quiet for what seemed like a long time. "I'm hungry. Let's eat and then you can take me home. I want to change clothes."

"After that, will you come with me to see Wes?"

Mary touched his chin as though she was fascinated with his stubble—with him. "Of course. But only if you shave first. I don't want everyone in town to think I have a scruffy boyfriend."

His eyebrows shot up at her use of the quaint term. "Am I your boyfriend?"

Grabbing his hand, she dragged him inside toward the kitchen. "That's exactly what you are."

No. No he wasn't. He was a liar on a mission. And it was a frigging disaster that he couldn't tell her the damned truth.

"Too bad your mother wasn't at the farm while we were there this morning. I would've liked to meet her."

Not that Jake thought for one moment that Jolene Walsh would arrange to kill her own daughter. But she could very well be up to her neck in the money-laundering scheme. And, after all, that was what his investigation was all about.

Keeping his eyes on the road ahead, he waited for Mary's reply. He had several people in mind as potential suspects for involvement in the international money-laundering operation he'd been sent to Honey Creek to investigate. Jolene was only one of them.

Mary sat straight up in her seat. "You would like to meet my mom?" He could feel her grinning all the way across the front seats of his SUV. "I want you two to meet. But Mom usually works at the family business office in the mornings. In the afternoon, she takes care of Patrick, my brother Peter's little boy, after school. Maybe we can catch her at one place or the other later."

Jake nodded. He had a great interest in gaining access to the Walsh business offices. All he needed was a few minutes alone with one of their computers.

Pulling the SUV into the lot belonging to the sheriff's office, Jake noted that the small redbrick building, situated on the frontage road, was typical of small-town sheriffs' offices throughout the West.

"Are we sure Wes will be in?" Mary undid her seat belt and hesitated with her hand on the door handle.

"Yeah. I called his office while you were changing. The secretary…or dispatcher, whoever answered the phone, said he would be in the office doing paperwork all morning."

Mary opened her door, but Jake spoke before she could step out. "Wait there," he demanded.

She turned her head to look at him but he was already heading around the front of the truck. "It's the boyfriend's job to help his girlfriend out of the vehicle."

Mary laughed and the sound tingled inside his chest. "Vehicle? You sound like a cop. But I like the general idea."

He fitted his hands around her waist and lifted her to

the ground. Golden sunshine sparked in her hair on this cloudless day and made him think of burnished copper pans. The mere sight of her many ripe colors glowing in the sunlight made his gut tremble.

"Thank you," she told him demurely. "I've been on my own a long time. It may take me a while to get used to considering someone else."

"I'm not worried. We've got time." And he would burn in hell for that statement along with all the other lies.

Jake took her by the hand and marched toward Wes Colton's office. Somehow he was going to finish this investigation in record time, and Colton had best find his murderer in record time, too.

When Jake was ready to leave town and disappear back into covert life, he wanted no chance of Mary being hurt by some panicked murderer with nothing to lose. Everything had to be wrapped up here before he left.

Yeah? And how was he supposed to wrap up his love for her then? Not such a simple thing. Nearly impossible, in fact. Sighing inwardly, he supposed he wouldn't even bother to try. He'd better get used to the idea of living without her.

"I'll be back in a few minutes, Jake. I want to step outside and call my mother. I need to ask where we can meet her today."

Mary hesitated at the door to Wes Colton's office. She'd given him her statement. But she couldn't add much to what Jake had already told him. Neither of them had seen the driver of the truck or gotten a glimpse of the plates. Jake said the truck was probably long gone by now and Wes agreed.

Still, the idea that someone had tried to kill them occupied too much of her thoughts. Mary would much rather be thinking of Jake and trying to decide if they had a future together. She wished she could be like her sister and her best friend, holding back and not jumping ahead into a relationship too fast. But Jake kept spinning her head around with his kisses and those longing looks.

"That's fine, Mary." The reply came from Wes. "I have a couple more things to ask Jake anyway. But don't wander too far away from the front door."

"You think someone might try to hurt me here? Right in front of the sheriff's office?" She was aghast.

Wes opened his mouth, but Jake answered first. "No one knows. That's the whole point. When I'm not around, you watch out for yourself. Keep your eyes open, and try not to be alone for any longer than is necessary. I don't want anything happening to you."

She nodded at him and turned away. But his words made her feel stupidly happy as she stepped out into the brilliant, sunshine-filled day.

"So you believe your cover is blown?" Wes leaned back in his desk chair with a thoughtful look on his face.

The sheriff was taller and broader than Jake, and maybe a couple of years younger. But Jake's instincts told him Wes would turn out to be a good ally.

"Not necessarily," Jake hedged. "It's possible the assault was not about me, but it could've been someone who wants to harm Mary. I'm trying to get her to confide in me. Maybe somewhere in her subconscious she has information that could be dangerous to her."

Wes wiped his hand across his mouth as though his next words would be distasteful. "I'm not comfortable with you using Mary Walsh this way. It's obvious she's infatuated with you. You can see it in her eyes. And she…has no experience to fall back on.

"I've always liked Mary," Wes added. "I don't want to see her hurt."

"I like Mary, too," Jake told the sheriff truthfully. "A lot. I was deadly serious when I said I didn't want anything happening to her."

With elbows on his knees, Jake hung his head for a moment, trying to decide how much to tell Wes about his true feelings. "I've got a big problem with Mary, Colton. I care for her. I didn't mean to, but I…

"Well, let's just say she's special," he finished. "But I believe she is in real danger. I'm not sure whether I brought the trouble down on her or not." Like hell. He knew his presence in Honey Creek had contributed to Mary's troubles.

Wes shook his head; he wasn't as positive as Jake. "What's the problem? Tell her who you are and what you're doing in Honey Creek. You know she's not involved with either the murder or the money-laundering scheme. Maybe if you were truthful with her, she might be willing to help you."

"Believe me…" Jake pursed his lips to keep from shouting out his frustration at the situation.

He counted to ten and then said, "I've thought of that a thousand times over the past couple of days. But even if I broke cover for her, I know enough about Mary now to know she could never forgive the lies. I started out on the wrong foot with her—lying to her and keeping her in dark. And now I'm paying for it."

Wes took a deep breath. "I see. You do care for her and you're in a hard place right now. But when this assignment is over... What then?"

"Tell her the truth and beg her to forgive me." Jake opened his hands, palms up as though he needed forgiveness from the whole world. Maybe he did.

"She won't," he continued. "But at least I have to try. And in the meantime, I intend to protect her with my life."

"Yeah, that's a damned hard rock you're sitting on." The expression on Wes's face was sympathetic. "Can I do anything to help?"

"Find the murderer, Colton. I have a feeling he or she is the one also targeting Mary."

"You have any suggestions along that vein?"

Jake started to shake his head, but then he said, "It's occurred to me that if Mark Walsh was such a playboy, there might be a couple of spurned women out there who would gladly have taken his life."

"Yeah?" Wes made a note on the legal pad sitting on his desk. "Well, there're a few women right here in Honey Creek that had both a motive and the means."

Jake cleared his throat, knowing this one was going to be tough. "Have you considered Jolene Walsh as a murder suspect? I mean, talk about a woman spurned. Not to mention that she might be very glad to get rid of her supposedly dead husband in order to take up with his best friend."

Nodding, Wes said. "She's right on top of the list. But you haven't met her yet, have you?"

"Not yet."

"She's one of the least threatening people I've ever known." Wes chopped the air with his hand as if that was a pure truth. "Look, some members of my family have been pissed at her and Craig Warner for fifteen long years because of my brother Damien's incarceration. But I'm absolutely positive she had nothing to do with that one."

Wes tilted his head for a second as though he was considering his next words. "My gut says she didn't do the crime this time, either. But I intend to eliminate her as a suspect the right way. With facts. For your sake, I hope I'm right."

"For my sake?"

"I can't imagine how hard that would be—watching the woman you love find out her mother is a murderer."

Love. Jake had never mentioned the word but somehow Wes had known.

Wes was right. Seeing Mary's faith in her mother dissolve would be tough. Just as tough as if he proved Mary's mother was involved in racketeering and money-laundering.

Jake swallowed the truth down hard, and found himself wishing he was anywhere else but in the middle of this mission. It might cause the death of him yet.

Chapter 9

"I'm sorry, Mare." Craig Warner sat behind a desk piled high with work and looked up at Mary through reading glasses. "Your mother had to run a couple of errands and couldn't wait for you."

"But I talked to her on the phone a little while ago." Mary heard a whine in her voice and fought it. "And she said for us to meet her here at the office."

Disappointed, Mary sat against the armrest of a leather office chair and waited for Craig's explanation. Craig looked especially good today. His crisp navy-blue suit went well with his salt-and-pepper hair and chestnut-brown eyes. But he was such a dear that she thought it could be his warm goodwill making him look so handsome.

Mary wasn't sure what she would've done without Craig Warner after her father had supposedly died the first time. He'd stepped up and became a father figure to all the Walsh kids. If only he'd been her real father, her whole life would've been much different.

Craig folded his hands on the desk and looked over the rim of his glasses. "Your mom won't be too long. But she wanted to know if you and your…friend…would like to join us for lunch today. We're both eager to meet him." Craig looked behind her toward the open door. "Where is he?"

"Jake's waiting in Mom's office. I didn't want to miss her in case she was only across the way at the brewery and would be right back. I figured we'd catch her one place or the other."

Craig nodded. "Listen, it's almost noon. Why don't the three of us ride out to the farm together to meet your mother? Your friend Susan should be delivering a catered lunch for all of us about now."

"Oh, yum. I love Susan's cooking." Things were definitely looking up. "Will she still be there when we arrive?"

"No, sorry again. Susan said she had a million things to do today. You'll have to settle for your mother and me."

Mary chuckled, glad that she had so many people in her life that loved her. Her mother, Craig, Susan…and now Jake?

He had not said a word about love. But perhaps that was one of those *man* things she still didn't understand. Of course, she hadn't told him she loved him, either. Mary felt unsure of herself—of him.

Well, she tried to think on the bright side, he was here now. If it didn't last, she would be okay. She hoped. But meanwhile, she intended to take advantage of him—every chance she got.

Jake barely had the time to replace the back of the computer before Mary and Craig came to get him for lunch. He'd managed to plant a wireless transmitter that could access all the computers in the office. His partner could capture not only everything now on the computer's hard drive, but also everything placed on it at a later date.

This part of his mission had taken a court order, but Jake had no intention of announcing that fact to the potential suspects. He also had another court order in his pocket for planting a transmitter in a different office in another part of Honey Creek. But he wasn't even close to figuring out how to access that one yet.

"It's really nice to meet you, son." Craig Warner gave him a curt smile and shook his hand. "I'm sorry Jolene isn't here, but she can't wait to meet you. Are you ready for a fantastic lunch?"

"I'm always ready to eat, sir. Is Mary's mother a good cook?" He took a deep breath and smelled the pervasive odor of hops coming from the brewery. That sweet molasseslike smell was hard to miss.

Both Mary and Craig laughed at his question and he noted both their eyes crinkled at the corners in the same way. They didn't look like father and daughter, but many of their mannerisms were the same.

"My mother can barely boil water," Mary told him. "But she has other good qualities."

Jake chuckled along with them, trying to match his demeanor to theirs. "Well, then, who's cooking the meal?" He hoped it wouldn't be him. He needed the time to do a little covert snooping and for asking pointed questions.

"Come on," Mary said as she took his arm. "We'll tell you all about it on the way."

Sitting across the table from Craig and Jolene, Jake paid close attention to them for any deception cues. But so far, neither had showed any of the usual signs. He wasn't a world-class detector of liars like those on TV, but he'd been trained by the best of them. With these two suspects, he hadn't noticed even one sweaty palm nor had either touched their forehead tentatively. They never even looked down into their plates. Not once, through the entire long lunch and conversation afterward. They'd both been all smiles and appeared to be trying to please their daughter's new lover. If one or both of them was a liar, they were damned good at it.

Jake kept the conversation steered in the direction of Mark Walsh's murder. Everyone at the table had an opinion to share on the subject of Mark Walsh. But Craig and Jolene were not as gracious as Mary had been on the subject of the dead man. Still, neither of them seemed to hate the man enough to murder him.

The longer he sat with Craig and Jolene and enjoyed their company, the more he was coming to believe Wes Colton's declaration. Jolene Walsh possessed a nonthreatening personality. In some ways she reminded him of Mary. Sweet. Unassuming. Intelligent. But without her daughter's biting wit and sure mind.

He could easily picture Mark Walsh or someone else just as strong manipulating her into assisting with a money-laundering scheme.

As he studied her, he noted that Jolene also had the

same coloring as her daughter. Mary's earnest amber eyes and long red hair were mirrored in the woman sitting across the table. But unlike Mary's, Jolene's beauty was delicate. Almost vulnerable.

On the other hand, Craig seemed happy enough with Jolene. Every once in a while in the middle of the conversation, Craig's hand would sneak over and give Jolene's hand a tender squeeze.

Jake was about to come to the conclusion that if anyone in this room could've been a murderer, it was Craig. Passion swam in Craig's eyes whenever he looked at Jolene. And Jake knew extreme passion could sometimes be a precursor to violence.

Despairing of ever learning anything helpful to his mission from this couple, he said, "It's been a terrific lunch. But don't you two have to return to work?"

"I'm due to babysit my grandson this afternoon after school." Jolene beamed as though the idea itself was as grand as the boy. "I'll drop Craig off at the office on my way into town."

Jolene scooted her chair back and stood before either Craig or himself could assist her. "Mary, before I leave," she said, "I'd like to show you a couple of outfits that I bought for you today. Can you come with me to your bedroom?"

Mary raised her eyebrows as though the idea of new clothes was a surprise, but she followed her mother down the hall.

"I'm glad we have a moment alone, Jake." Craig stood next to the table beckoning Jake to follow him into the family room.

Jake figured this was going to be yet another lecture

about not hurting Mary similar to the one Wes had given. He was ready for it. Deserved it.

Craig sat on the sofa and Jake sat in the lone armchair across from him.

"Mary's mother and I are pleased by your attention to her daughter," Craig began as he leaned forward. "It's time Mary found someone. Jolene once imagined her youngest daughter might never find anyone who would appreciate how special she is. Your appearance at this critical time is almost too good to be true."

Jake nodded but could hear the *but* in Craig's voice and knew what was coming next. "Yes, sir. Mary has grown to mean a lot to me in the short time I've known her."

"Yes, I'm seeing that in your eyes whenever you look at her. That's why I think you should know something about her past that she might not be willing to share."

Uh-oh, this lecture was going to start with the our-daughter-is-a-virgin speech.

Jake tried to head it off. "It's not necessary. But thanks for the thought anyway. I believe it would be better if Mary tells me whatever she wants me to know." That sounded like something a loyal boyfriend would say, didn't it?

"In most cases I would agree with you, son. But Mary may not even be admitting this to herself. You see, Mark Walsh was…"

Jake held his tongue and waited for the *a difficult man* comment. But he didn't get it.

"A bastard. And a terrible father. Especially to the two girls. When they were young, before he disappeared, Mark would take every opportunity to belittle them in public. Make them look small and appear to be selfish brats when they were anything but. And I'm fairly positive he also terrorized them at home."

"He was abusive?"

Craig shook his head softly. "I could never prove any physical abuse. Mary and Lucy never showed any marks and neither ever spoke up. But I'm sure he emotionally stunted both of them."

"Did Jolene ever mention problems at home? Why didn't she do something to stop it?"

"I don't think Jolene actually knew what was going on when she wasn't around. She always worked long hours at the brewery and I believe she may have closed her eyes to what her husband was doing. Both inside and outside the house.

"It's Mary that I have always worried about the most," Craig continued. "Puberty is hard enough to live through without having the person who you most want to love you chipping away at your self-esteem day after day. Mary took it the hardest. She withdrew into her books and found comfort in food. And I..."

Craig hesitated, took a deep breath of air. "I couldn't save her. By the time Mark disappeared it was too late for Mary. By then, none of us could reach inside her shell."

Jake was taken aback for the moment, then it began to make sense. "She said she went to a shrink for help losing weight. Did she go for more than that?"

"I'm sure she did. She's changed a lot in the past few years. Gotten stronger, more self-assured. I hardly ever see that frightened look in her eyes anymore."

Shaken, Jake didn't want to consider what Mary's secret background could mean for his mission. Or what his mission might mean to Mary's well-being when it was over—and he was long gone.

He stood on shaky legs but managed to speak in a strong voice. "Thank you. I'll keep what you said to myself, but I appreciate the heads-up."

"I love Mary, Jake. I love all the Welsh siblings as if they were my own children. But Mary has always been the most emotionally fragile. She seems happy for the first time that I can remember and I don't want any big surprises to come between you."

If Craig only knew, Jake thought sullenly. The biggest surprise of all was yet to come. A terrible storm cloud brewed on their horizon. And there was not a single thing he could think of to stop it.

Mary tilted her head to look at Jake's profile as he drove the SUV back home. She was so pleased with how the afternoon had turned out that she wanted to shout it to the world. Her mother and Craig had gone out of their way to make Jake feel at home and welcome.

The only small glitch in her day had come when her mother had reminded her to go slow with Jake. Jolene told the story of her own first love affair, and how that had been a whirlwind romance, too. It was how she'd ended up with Mark Walsh.

Yes, that none-too-subtle reminder had definitely rained on Mary's good mood. But she'd already been thinking along those same lines. The only problem with going slow was that when she and Jake were together, her mind seemed to take a nap. From there, her body jumped ahead and did all the racing.

As she stared over at him now, she realized that Jake didn't look pleased at all. He clenched and unclenched his jaw. A vein stood out at his temple. Was he mad at her for some reason? Mary felt a shudder of panic, wondering if Craig had said something while she'd been out of the room.

"Are you okay?" she asked, not knowing how else to start.

"What?" He slipped her a glance. "Oh, sure. I'm concerned about an alarm system for the house, is all. I called and they can't send anyone out here right away."

She heaved a relieved sigh. "I suppose you could stay at the farm until the system is installed—if you want. I'm sure my mom wouldn't mind." Mary hoped Jake would say no, but she'd needed to make the offer.

A chuckle rumbled up in his throat. "And you would be staying in your bedroom and I could stay in the guest room? Is that what you want?"

She shook her head vigorously enough that it nearly flew off her neck. "No!"

He removed one hand from the wheel and intertwined his fingers with hers. "Thank God."

After that, his expression lightened. The lines across his forehead relaxed and the corners of his mouth curved up in one of his charming smiles.

Mary would've dearly loved to lean over and plant a kiss on each of those corners. And on a lot of other places as well. It was a good thing they were almost at Jake's house.

Clearing her throat, she forced herself to think about another subject in the meantime. "Remember when I was talking about you coming to one of Mom's parties? Well, guess what? Mom came up with the same idea. I didn't even have to mention it to her."

Jake nodded absently. "That sounds nice. When would it be?"

"Tomorrow night. She wants to throw a big barbecue out in the farmyard and invite most of the town to meet you. You don't mind, do you?"

"Not at all. I'm one of the best grilling chefs you'll ever meet. Barbecue is one of my specialties."

He hesitated for a second as he maneuvered the SUV into his long driveway. Then he added, "That also means I have you all to myself for tonight—and nothing could make me happier."

The look in his eyes as he'd made that comment was unmistakable. Heat ran along her nerve endings and nearly boiled the blood in her veins.

Okay, she thought as she jumped out of the SUV and headed for the front of the house. Now she really couldn't wait to get inside.

Still conflicted about his role in Mary's life, Jake barricaded them inside the house and fought his hormones. All afternoon and through the early evening he distracted them both in the kitchen with talk of the upcoming barbecue and with testing good grilling sauces and rubs.

All that time, Mary kept making it very clear what she would rather be doing. He was right there with her in spirit, but he wasn't sure his conscience could take much more.

Then a little while ago, Mary had disappeared. At first he hadn't been too worried. But he'd only now noticed she was being too quiet and started to worry. She'd better not have left the house. In his gut he could feel the danger lurking outside in the dark woods.

After checking the doors and both wings of the house for any sign of her, Jake reluctantly climbed the stairs. How could he ever hope to resist her? There was no hope.

Deep in his psyche, he knew what was right and what was wrong. And he'd been wrong since the very first night they had ever made love. To keep on making the same mistake over and over seemed insane.

But that was just it. He'd lost his mind where Mary was concerned. In the middle of a mission he'd begun to wish he was in another occupation. Anything else. Covert work had long ago lost its appeal. Now he couldn't wait to forget the Bureau and everything it had come to represent. If only he had changed jobs before he'd met Mary.

Knowing he was thinking crazy thoughts, Jake hit the top of the stairs trying to find some logical excuse for not sleeping in the same bed with her. His hands fisted at the mere thought.

After peeking into a couple of spare bedrooms, he found them as empty as he'd imagined. At last, he lightly pushed open the master bedroom door and prayed he would find her fast asleep on the king-size bed.

The sheets had been turned down, but Mary was nowhere in sight. Then he heard the shower running. He frowned at the bathroom door and his mind drifted into some kind of trance.

He walked toward heaven, shedding his clothes as he went. It was too late for him. Now that he'd tasted her, he couldn't stay away. No other woman had ever made him this hungry. This desperate.

Naked, he eased open the bathroom door. "Mary?" When he got no response, he walked over to the shower, pulled back the curtain and stepped in beside her.

"Jake! You scared me. Is anything wro—?"

He cut off her words by taking hold of her shoulders and lasering a kiss across her lips. Startled, she squeaked under his demanding moves. Almost immediately though, her body turned to soft, warm butter and she threw her arms around his neck.

Yes, he thought. They needed each other tonight. Why keep fighting it?

Deepening the kiss, he felt his heart racing as he turned his back to the warm spray and hugged her closer. Her skin was smooth. Wet. Hot. When she flattened her breasts against his chest and curled one long leg around one of his, Jake's body went impossibly hard.

Dragging her mouth from his, she looked at him with burning, bright eyes. "Help me. I don't know what to do."

He folded his hands under her bottom and backed them both up to the tile. "Wrap your legs around my waist, I'll do the rest."

As he entered her in one swift move, her moans echoed off the bathroom walls. Her head fell back and she tightened her legs around him, making the taut, sweet sensation of being inside her nearly unbearable.

He nipped at her neck, feeling the fire race under his skin. Her fingernails bit into his shoulders as he thrust once. And again. And again.

Too close to hold off any longer, Jake was grateful when her shudder rolled through him and her body pulsated around him. With a groan, he followed her over with one last thrust.

Gasping for air, he let her loose to slide down his

body and find her footing on the porcelain tub. But he kept his arms tightly around her as she sagged against him.

Reaching through the steamy spray, he turned off the water, but held her close for one more beat of his heart. Then he gathered her up in his arms and took her to his bed.

Outside in the dark, under a canopy of pines, the man known as the Pro trained his night-vision goggles on the second floor. Piece of cake.

His efforts of earlier this morning were about to pay off big. No one inside had any inkling of the danger they were in.

The new little game he was playing with them had turned out to be fun after all. Scaring a lawman off would take more than a couple of attempts. But this attempt would be a masterpiece.

Another couple of hours to wait. To be sure they were fast asleep.

Fingering the special cell phone he carried in his pocket, the Pro could hardly wait to place the call. The target would never know what had hit him. All of a sudden hell would surround the two of them in a wall of flames.

Maybe the guy would escape. Or maybe he wouldn't. The Pro didn't much care one way or the other.

Chapter 10

Jake watched as Mary crept down the stairs in front of him. It was late and they'd deliberately left off all the lights. He would've much preferred to still be in their warm bed. But not Mary.

"Come on," she whispered with a giggle. "I'm starving. We forgot to eat dinner."

"Late-night snacking isn't good for you." It was a half-baked attempt at coaxing her back to bed, but he knew it wouldn't work.

"You're as bad as my therapist. All right, I'll eat celery and run an extra mile tomorrow. I just need something in my stomach or I won't sleep." She wrapped his terry robe tighter around her waist and went up on tiptoes to dance down the stairs.

"We could turn on the lights," he grumbled.

"This way is more fun. I guess you've never been to a slumber party."

Yes, he had. Every time they slept together was a party. He was becoming more and more addicted to it every day.

Grateful that he'd stopped upstairs long enough to put on a pair of jeans, Jake wished he'd also taken the time to slip into a pullover sweater. It was damned cold in here.

Mary was nearing the bottom of the stairs when she stopped dead. "I smell…"

In the glow coming from the kitchen nightlights, Jake saw Mary turning back to him. "It smells like smoke in here," she whispered.

"Maybe it's coming from outside. Sometimes the wind shifts and the scent of a neighbor's chimney smoke seeps in late at night."

"No…" Mary tentatively stepped down on the wood-planked floor.

She looked to the right, toward the kitchen and the western wing of the house. Then, she turned left.

"Jake, something's on fire! I see smoke in the family room."

She'd already taken two steps toward the family room before it hit him and he pulled her backward. "Don't go any farther. Run back upstairs, get your cell phone and call the fire department."

"We have 911 service," she said without hesitation. "I'll call."

As she passed him on the way up the stairs, he made a few more demands. "Put on your shoes and grab your purse. Come back downstairs in less than three minutes. It's important."

"But I don't see any flames."

"Just do it."

She nodded and flew up the stairs. Before she was even out of sight, Jake was on his way to the kitchen to retrieve the weapon he had secreted in a floor safe under the stove. He would rather Mary not see where and how he'd hidden the .38, but knew he needed to be armed.

After taking the weapon in hand, he hurriedly checked the chambers. Before his next breath, a small explosion rocked the house. *Mary!* Shoving the .38 into his waistband, he ran toward the sound, praying the explosion had not been on the second floor.

"Jake!"

He saw Mary, stopped on the staircase and staring wide-eyed toward the floor below her. Flames shot outward from the family room toward the stairs and front door. Rivers of fire licked at the bottom of the stairs where she stood.

He opened his mouth to tell her to stay where she was and he would come for her, but she turned and ran back up the stairs before he could get the words out. "Mary, no!" he called after her.

Jake tried to follow her, but blasts of heat and a rain of cinders threatened to sear his clothing. Turning on his heels, he dashed back into the kitchen, put a wet rag to his nose and pulled a ten-pound bag of flour out of the pantry. Back at the stairs, he began pouring the flour on each stair, dousing flames as he went. He tried to keep from succumbing to panic, worrying about Mary upstairs on her own. He had to get to her.

As he began making a dent in the blaze on the lower stairs, Mary appeared right above him. She was covered head to toe by a wet blanket and held another in her hands.

"Here." She bunched up the blanket and threw it down the stairs toward him. Then she covered her face and made a dash for it.

In the distance, Jake could hear a siren. Another soon joined the screeching sounds of the first.

Mary's shoes hit the floor at the bottom of the stairs as she grabbed him by the arm. "Cover up and let's get out of here," she shouted.

Like dozens of tiny fireflies, sparks from the inferno in the family room swirled around in a breeze that had to be coming from an open window. But he hadn't left any windows open or unlocked.

Sounds of the holocaust grew deafening in his ears. Snapping and popping, flames raced along the floorboards and up the walls in fiery ribbons. Smoke curls glided through the air, floating into other rooms and heading up the stairs like living, breathing intruders.

Mary tugged at his arm. "Come on." She started for the front door, but Jake dug in his heels.

She swung on him and a muffled cry reached his ears from under her blanket. "What's the matter with you?"

Wrapping the blanket around his shoulders, he withdrew his .38. "We can't run straight out the front door," he yelled. "It could be an ambush."

"What?" Her eyes opened wide at the sight of the .38. "No way."

He pulled her close, tucked her under the cover of his arm, and headed for the kitchen door. When they reached it, he dragged Mary along with him, flattening them both to the protection of the wall beside the door.

Then he chanced a look outside, searching the grounds nearby. This section of the land had once been used as a kitchen garden and an old six-foot fence protected the entire area. From what he could see in the dark, no one was lying in wait for them within the garden fence.

Clear air prevailed on this side of the house, too. His gut told him the fire must be contained to the family room and the eastern wing of the house. Meanwhile, sirens wailed through the starry night, growing closer by the second. The sounds gave him hope of making it outside without a sniper picking them off.

Tugging Mary along with him, Jake chanced it and dashed for the garden gate. By the time he had unlatched the gate and hidden the weapon under his shirt, blue and white strobe lights were lighting up the entire night sky. Honey Creek's volunteer fire department vehicles and sheriff's cars were already on the scene.

Jake finally relaxed enough to let go of Mary and the two of them ran out to meet the firemen. Fire trucks had already been set up and the firemen were preparing to roll out the hose from one of the pumper trucks.

A pretty blonde woman in a heavy fireman's jacket and hard hat greeted them in the front yard. "Are you hurt? Is anyone else in the house?"

"We were alone and I think we're both okay, Melissa." Mary swiveled to Jake. "You're not burned, are you?"

He coughed and felt his lungs screaming in protest.

"Come with me," the blonde told him. "A little oxygen should help that cough."

"I don't need oxygen. I want to help with the fire."

"Me, too," Mary chimed in. "What can we do?"

The blonde woman studied him up and down and

seemed to come to a decision. "Let's go check with the chief. He's manning the com system."

Within two hours, the fire chief was sifting through ashes inside the still-smoldering remains of the family room. Accompanied by the sheriff, Jake stepped carefully through charred ruins to join him.

Glancing over his shoulder, Jake checked on Mary. She sat on the back of one of the fire trucks with a Mylar blanket over her shoulders, while someone poured her a hot drink from a thermos. The blonde, Melissa Kelley, stood beside her. It turned out that Melissa was a volunteer paramedic for the Honey Creek fire department and the sister of Mary's best friend Susan.

Jake's mind flashed back a couple of hours to Mary, her image reflected by the raging blaze, as she'd used a garden hose to wet down the perimeter of the house. Hot and grimy, Mary had been absolutely spectacular in her borrowed equipment as she'd fought to keep the blaze from spreading.

She was sure something. Not once during the entire emergency had she complained or been too scared to help. An impressive strength of spirit came shining through her otherwise timid and studious demeanor. Jake was impressed by her actions and by her bravery in the face of danger.

He'd thought before that he was falling in love, but now he was hopeless. He had never met anyone like her and doubted he ever would.

"What do you think, little brother?" Wes asked the fire chief when they came close enough to speak.

"Arson. No question." The chief turned to Jake, removed his glove and shook his hand. "Name's Perry

Colton. Wes tells me you and Mary Walsh just made it out with your lives."

Another Colton brother. Jake sifted through his memories of the family's facts. He recollected six Colton brothers altogether. Most of them were not under suspicion, and like Wes, Perry Colton was definitely one of the Coltons he'd put in the cleared column.

"I wanted to thank you for your help manning one of the fire hoses," Perry continued. "It's summer and a few of our volunteers are out of town on vacation. We're a little short-handed and it was a blessing that you stepped in."

"No problem." Jake looked around at the charred walls. "How bad was it?"

Perry turned, scanning the scene. "The bulk of the damage was confined to the family room. The blaze was set by someone who knew what they were doing. But whoever did it wasn't aiming to take down the entire house."

Rubbing the back of his neck, Perry continued speaking over his shoulder. "The upstairs is relatively untouched. Not even much smoke damage. The kitchen doesn't smell wonderful, but it should be easy enough to clean up once the rest of the house is secured. Looks to me like someone was only trying to make a point."

Twisting back, Perry confronted Jake. "You have any idea what that point might've been?"

Wes stepped in between them and his tone of voice became more professional than the one he had been using. "Are you personally going to collect the arson evidence? Or are you planning on calling in the state investigators?"

Perry stared at his brother with speculation raging

in his eyes. "You know something about this you're not saying, Wes?"

Wes's fists went to his hips. "Listen, Perry, just do your…"

Jake put his hand on Wes's chest to keep him from saying anything more, then turned back to address Perry. "There'll be a special investigation team coming in later this morning to secure the rest of the house and clean up the mess. It would be helpful if you could keep the entire area clear of sightseers until then."

The understanding expression on Wes's face and the way he backed up half a step meant he would defer to the FBI in talking to the fire chief. On the other hand, Perry wasn't ready to concede anything.

"Special investigation team?" Perry's eyes narrowed. "This team gonna have some kind of identification they can give me? Who are you anyway?"

"No one who matters," Jake said in the friendliest tone he could manage. "The team will carry ID—for your eyes only. But nothing they can show for general public consumption. Meanwhile, the sheriff will vouch for me and I would take it as a personal favor if you could keep the team's work here quiet. They'll arrive looking like a regular damage cleanup and alarm-system crew.

"It would also be great," Jake tacked on. "If you could tell the media that on first glance this fire looks accidental."

"We don't have a big media presence here," Perry told him. "Just the Honey Creek *Gazette*. And I think I can hold off the editor for the time being."

"I'd appreciate it." Jake started to walk away but turned back first. "Thanks for everything, chief. Fire-fighting is one hell of an occupation. Thank God there are volunteers in the world like you."

Jake shook Perry's hand again, nodded to Wes and headed off to check on Mary. He could imagine the sort of questions he would be facing from her. But the biggest problem remained. What answers would he, could he, give?

"You're sure your mother doesn't mind if I change clothes at the farm? I'm pretty grungy." Jake drove down the long driveway toward the farm as the sun broke through the clouds at midmorning.

"*You're* grungy?" Mary tried not to touch anything inside Jake's SUV. "Look at me. I have twigs and knots in my hair that may never come out. My clothes and shoes are hopeless and will have to be pitched. And I smell like the inside of a chimney. If she finds out, Mom shouldn't care which of us makes the biggest mess."

She'd tried to convince Jake to let someone else drive her home, but he wouldn't hear of it. Ever since the fire had broken out last night, he'd been keeping her in sight constantly.

Mary wanted to believe his motives were pure. That he had been disturbed by the fire and by his fear of her being killed, and he'd needed to keep her nearby in order to assure himself of her safety.

She wanted to believe that.

But then she remembered how he'd magically produced a gun last night and had looked very much like someone who knew how to use it. Curiosity sneaked into her mind at odd moments and caused her extreme anxiety. Why hadn't he told her about the gun before?

Mary tried to talk to him about it earlier. But he'd put her off, saying he didn't want to talk around strangers.

So, she tried again. "You never explained where the gun came from last night. And where is it now? Did you leave it back in the house?"

Jake set his jaw for a moment and she was afraid he wouldn't talk to her. Finally he said, "I keep a gun for protection. It's fairly isolated out there where I live."

"It's isolated here at the farm, too," she argued as he pulled up in the front yard. "But we don't have any guns.

"Well, I have to take that back," she said as she remembered the facts. "We do have a couple of shotguns that the boys used to scare foxes away from the chickens. But I keep forgetting about those. I haven't seen them in years."

He parked the SUV and turned off the engine. As she opened her mouth to ask something else, he hopped out and came around the front to her side.

When he opened her door, she asked point-blank, "Jake, where is the gun now?"

"In the duffel I packed before we left the house."

"Here? You brought a gun along with us? But why?"

"It's for protection, Mary. And I didn't want to explain it to the firemen or anyone else who might be digging around inside the house today."

Shaking her head in disbelief, she slid out of the seat and headed toward her front door. Something was just not right about what he'd said. She could tell he was leaving something out—something big.

Mary needed time alone to think things over. They'd been through a lot together. She didn't want to believe

Jake was doing something wrong. But the truth was, he could be involved in anything. He could be a criminal for all she knew.

A shiver went through her as she unlocked the door and let them inside. By the time they reached the living room, she was already praying that she was wrong. If he wasn't exactly who he said he was, then he had to be lying. Maybe about a lot of things.

And she couldn't stand that idea. Please, no. Not Jake.

A short while after she got him situated in the guest bathroom with towels and soap, Mary stripped and stood under a cold shower spray in her own bathroom. She didn't want to think about Jake, but that seemed to be the only thing on her mind.

What was she going to do about him? How did she really feel about him?

Unfortunately, her heart formed a loud and clear answer. She was falling in love with him, despite all her heroic efforts not to rush. She probably had been in love with him from that very first night and had been lying to herself about it all along.

But right from the beginning she had also known he was keeping something from her. She'd thought it might be because he was already married. Making love to a married man would've been disastrous enough. Now she had to wonder if the man could be a criminal of some sort. Perhaps a murderer?

Rubbing shampoo through her hair, Mary considered all she knew of Jake. Her facts were slim. But the feelings...the warm feelings in her heart could be counted in the billions.

She knew it didn't matter as much about the gun.

Jake was a good man deep inside. She couldn't be in love with a criminal. No way.

Mary rinsed off, still trying to make sense of her emotions. She didn't want to fall for a man she didn't really know. It wasn't smart. She could be left hurt and humiliated in the end.

Grabbing a towel and wrapping her wet hair, she came to the conclusion that she needed advice. From her friends. And from her family. She simply wasn't thinking clearly.

"You've got to be kidding," Jake said with a chuckle. "Your mother still plans on throwing us a barbecue tonight? Haven't we had enough of smoke to last us for a while?"

She planted her hands on her hips. "Ha. We have to eat, don't we? And you said your kitchen won't be back in shape for cooking until tomorrow. I don't think Mom heard about the fire, but still, it was nice of her to offer."

Jake needed time alone. He'd been badly shaken by the fire and didn't want anyone to know it. He'd hoped to leave Mary safely with her family tonight while he went back to work on the house. The FBI security team out of Denver was already there, gathering evidence and securing the undamaged parts of the house. He wanted to help with the boarding-up of windows and doors. To clean up the soot. To be alone with his thoughts and daydream about kicking an imaginary arsonist in the balls.

Mary was in far too much danger while she was with him. And she was beginning to ask difficult questions.

He'd reached a point where he needed a few moments of time-out to consider what to do about her.

What he preferred to do was to love her. Protect her. Keep her with him forever. But none of that was going to happen.

Still, he could not keep putting her into the line of fire. Even if that meant telling her the truth, breaking his cover and forfeiting his mission. He knew the truth would likely mean the end of their relationship. Mary would never accept his lies. Not even if they had been told as part of the job.

Jake had much to consider.

"I guess a barbecue will be okay," he hedged. "What'll we have to do to prepare?"

"Not a thing. My mom, Craig and Susan will handle everything. Mom'll be arriving soon to get started."

Jake couldn't think of any good reason to leave Mary here while he went off to think. "Uh. You look tired. Maybe you should catch a nap this afternoon. We didn't get much sleep."

"I'm not tired. But I do need a favor. My hair is an impossible mess. Can you drive me into town to get my hair done?"

"Sure. How long will that take?"

Mary ran her fingers through her hair and frowned down at the fringy ends. "Days. Maybe weeks." Then she laughed. "Just joking. Don't look so horrified. But I will be at the salon for several hours. Do you mind finding something else to do on your own?"

"Not at all." Perfect, he thought.

The two of them were in absolute sync. When

he'd needed time, she needed time. Two hearts magically beating as one? Naw. Too poetic for an undercover agent.

Chapter 11

Mary couldn't wait to close the door to Salon Allegra behind her. Eve Kelley had been cutting her hair for as long as she could remember. But all of a sudden Mary wasn't comfortable in the woman's shop anymore.

It seemed as though Mary wasn't comfortable in her own skin anymore. She'd begun scrutinizing every person she met in the course of her daily life. It was as if everyone in town, everyone she had known her whole life, could be lying.

Whenever she saw anyone, the first thing she did was wonder what they might know about the fire at Jake's. Or—whether they'd been in on her father's murder.

Drawing in a deep breath, Mary let the warmth of a late-afternoon sun temporarily melt away all her suspicions. She turned, but stopped before she could take the first step. Jake was waiting there, leaning casually against a light pole about five feet down the sidewalk.

"You look beautiful," he said without moving. "How do you feel?"

She felt like a woman in love who had reason to stop trusting her man. To stop trusting everybody. That was how she felt.

But she wasn't ready to say anything about it. "I'm okay. How about you? Any aftereffects from the smoke?"

Jake closed the gap between them and took her by the shoulders. "I don't know. I haven't been breathing all day—not until just now. Having you back in my arms has restarted my heart."

He bent his head, touching his lips to hers. His kiss wasn't passionate or as desperate as many of their kisses. But it was so tender and so meaningful that when he finally pulled away and gazed down at her, Mary's eyes were overflowing with unshed tears and her heart was overflowing, too.

Here was something she could trust. Whatever hidden agendas might lie between them, their need for each other seemed sincere and strong. The two of them had no problems in the bedroom—or the family room, or the kitchen—or wherever they could find a quiet place to be alone together.

So why was she ready to tell him goodbye? It seemed crazy. But on occasion she could swear Jake's eyes held the very same message that filled her heart. That the two of them were only together on borrowed time.

Sighing, she took a shaky step back and broke the spell. Just in time.

"Yoo-hoo. Is that you, Mary Walsh?"

Talk about being a little crazy. Maisie Colton appeared out of nowhere and headed straight down the sidewalk toward them. Caught between Jake and the town's weirdest citizen, Mary felt as if she were drowning in quicksand.

Shifting to the other foot, she mentally prepared for the upcoming blast of nuttiness.

"I thought that must be you," Maisie said as she came within striking distance. "But I could hardly believe my eyes. The formerly chubby little Mary Walsh kissing a strange man in public—and in broad daylight, no less. Who would've thought it? Strange happenings keep on coming in this town."

Mary closed her eyes and wished she could fly away.

"The name's Jake Pierson, ma'am." Jake's mellow voice punctured Maisie's screeching and worked like a salve on Mary's nerves. "And it was me who was kissing the gorgeous Miss Walsh, not the other way around," he finished.

Mary's eyes popped open when she heard Jake's words. He stepped in close to her side and folded her arm around his elbow as though they belonged together.

"How very gallant of you, Jake. And I'm Maisie Colton. Of *the* Coltons, you know?"

"Uh-huh. I've already met several of your brothers."

"Oh, them. Bo-o-o-ring." Maisie waved away any more talk of her family. "I was hoping to run into you two. I need your help."

Mary's mouth dropped open. She didn't even like guessing what Maisie might want from them. Eleven years older than Mary, Maisie Colton had meant trouble for as long as Mary could remember. Though she was certainly beautiful, tall, thin, and with startling aqua eyes, in a way, Maisie reminded Mary of one of the witches from the book *The Witches of Eastwick*. Beautiful but deadly.

"I heard about your house burning last night, Jake. Too bad. What—or who—do you suppose could've started it?"

Jake's eyes narrowed slightly as he regarded her. "The fire started in the family room near the fireplace. Fireplaces are known to be an accident waiting to happen."

Mary heard the hedge in Jake's words and wondered if Maisie noticed it, too.

"Right," Maisie said as she flipped her hair. "Well, I called the *Dr. Sophie* TV show again this morning because I figured arson would be the thing that would tip the scales in favor of them doing a piece on Honey Creek for a national audience."

Yep. Maisie had noted Jake's equivocation.

No one else might've caught it, but Mary saw that Jake was having a strange reaction to Maisie's ravings. He straightened up, the corners of his mouth tensed and he took a step back. Jake wasn't happy.

"Did the show seem interested *this* time, Maisie?" Mary wanted Jake to understand that the nutty woman had contacted the show many times in the past with her wild stories. "The last time you called, didn't they ask you not to contact them anymore?"

Maisie's shoulders slumped. "They said the same thing this time. But one of these days they will pay attention to me. Honey Creek is a hotbed of drama. I mean, really. First a murder, then that attack on your friend Susan a few weeks ago, last night's fire and now the town's former wild child has come back to town. We need something like the *Dr. Sophie* show to open things up around here and make people notice."

"What wild child?" Mary was stumped. "What on earth are you talking about?"

"Why, Mary, you should know. The library has supposedly hired Lily Masterson to be your new boss. Can you imagine? Lily Masterson, of all people. I thought we'd seen the last of her years ago."

Jake took Mary's arm and spun them in the other direction on the sidewalk. "Nice meeting you, Maisie. Mary and I are late. We'll see you around."

He whispered in Mary's ear. "Hope you don't mind me being rude to her, but…"

Mary chuckled. "Don't worry about it. Everyone in town knows she's a little unhinged. She's a single mother, and I pity her son. Poor kid is growing up way too soon, what with trying to compensate for his mother."

"How old is he?"

"Around fourteen. Kinda gawky for a teenager, but he's a really nice kid."

Jake made a couple of mental connections and since they were out of earshot, said, "Do you think it's possible she's just crazy enough to kill your father?"

"Definitely. The woman can be downright spooky. I would have to put her up at the top of any possible list of suspects."

Jake wouldn't go that far. He didn't consider Maisie a serious suspect. In his experience, being a little eccentric was not a prerequisite for a murderer. And inviting the media in to inspect your life usually meant you had nothing serious to hide.

But you never knew with nuts who craved publicity.

As they reached his SUV, Jake asked, "What was she saying about your friend being attacked a few weeks ago?"

Mary climbed into the passenger seat. "Susan was attacked by some weirdo. It turned out some man had been stalking her. She ended up in the hospital." Mary shook her head sadly as she buckled up. "The creep was apparently looking for revenge against Susan's new fiancé and put Susan in the middle."

"But she's okay? The stalker was caught, wasn't he?"

Mary nodded. "And everything is back to normal for Susan. Except now she's engaged to be married."

Jake climbed into the driver's seat and buckled in. He didn't want to keep talking about the town's domestic problems. He didn't want to talk about any sort of problems with Mary right now. She had unanswered questions in her mind about him carrying the weapon and warning her about a sniper while they tried to escape from a house fire. Too much discussion about other things might remind her of her doubts.

"I have good news," he said as he gave her a gentle look. "The house should be secured and cleaned up enough for us to stay there tonight. And your mother told me that her plans are all set for the barbecue. We're just going to make it back to the farm in time for last-minute preparations."

He'd been considering what to do about Mary all afternoon while working with the security-alarm team from Denver. But he hadn't yet come up with any specific plan.

Still, he knew things would soon be coming to a head. He'd even called his partner Jim and told him to stay close and be ready for anything.

Jake knew his cover had cracks as wide as the Grand Canyon, and things were closer than ever to the explosion point. More than anything, he needed to protect Mary from the fallout.

"You care about him. I can tell." Susan stood in the farm's kitchen, putting last-minute preparations together for the barbecue while she talked to Mary.

"Yeah, I do. I think I'm falling in love."

"But…" Susan's head shook and strands of her chin-length dark blond hair swung across her face. "What do you know of him? Wes said his background was okay, but what about the man's family?" She used her wrist to move the hair back.

"Jake told me his mother died when he was a kid and that he and his father are estranged. He said he doesn't have any brothers or sisters."

"How about ex-wives? Kids?"

Mary didn't like facing her worst fears. "He told me there weren't any ex-wives or kids, either."

"And you believe him? Guys can say whatever they want."

"How am I supposed to know for sure? He doesn't act like a liar." At least, not really. Mary could feel the tears threatening.

Susan stopped what she was doing and laid a hand on Mary's shoulder. "I don't mean to upset you right before your party, hon. Enjoy yourself and be happy. But tomorrow you and I need to get busy on the computer. We'll find out about his past. If we can't, we can always ask your brother Peter for help with a full investigation."

Mary sniffed and nodded her head. "Thanks. You're such a good friend. I didn't want to involve Peter, or you for that matter. But I don't know what else to do. Mom and Craig and Wes all seem to like Jake a lot. But..."

"I know. Here." Susan handed her a dish full of chicken pieces covered over with a film of clear plastic. "Help carry the meats out to the firepit. And try to forget about your worries at least for tonight. Tomorrow we'll find your answers about his personal life."

Mary nodded and headed for the door, but she couldn't forget. She couldn't forget anything when it came to Jake. Not the way he held her in his arms when the two of them made love. Nor the way he sometimes looked at her as though she had just made all his dreams come true. And she sure as heck couldn't get past the way his eyes sometimes brimmed over with secret pain.

Feeling a nasty ache of suspicion rising once more in her chest, Mary swallowed it down and stepped out into the late-afternoon sunlight. She hoped her fears would be put to rest tomorrow with a few simple strokes of the computer keys. But her gut told her not one thing about the man she loved was ever going to go down easy.

Jake manned one of the grills and kept an open can of beer at hand, trying to look casual. Every person in the entire crowd but one had been over to speak with him as the party carried on into the night. That should've been exactly the way he wanted it. But the one person missing was the only one he considered important. Mary.

She had been avoiding him all evening. Frustration at the impossible situation he'd created for himself quickly turned to outright panic at the thought of leaving her without protection. He couldn't let her simply walk away from him. Not until she understood the whole truth and could accept a bodyguard.

"Hi, Jake. Need any help?" Craig Warner ambled over wearing a barbecue chef's apron.

"No, thanks. Most of the cooking is over. I'll be looking for help with grill-cleaning duty pretty soon."

"I'll see if I can round someone up for you." Craig chuckled and rolled his eyes. "Have you managed to stay out of the way of all the gossip while cooking?"

Jake laughed. "Nope. I've spent most of the night listening to fantastic tales concerning both Maisie Colton and Lily Masterson, who I gather are unwed mothers with secret pasts. But I never would've imagined that a single difficult fact about a person's past would make them interesting enough to talk about for the rest of their lives."

"It shouldn't, but that's the way with small towns."

Jake threw Craig a quick look, then glanced absently back down at the burgers, blackening slowly on the grill. "Want to talk about something else for a change?" Without waiting for an answer, Jake went on, "A few of the people here tonight have hazarded a guess about who killed Mark Walsh. I think that's a question more interesting than gossiping about unwed mothers. Do you have any thoughts on the subject?"

"On who might've killed Mark? It's kind of amusing, actually." But Craig did not seem amused. "I probably have the strongest motives of anyone when you come to think of it."

"What motives are those?"

Craig shrugged a shoulder and looked around to see

if anyone else was close by. "Well, for one, I'm madly in love with his widow—and have been from the moment I first met her over thirty years ago."

"Yeah, I would consider that a good motive."

"You bet she is." Craig set his cup down and began ticking off reasons on his fingers. "For another thing, I could've killed Mark with my bare hands for the way he treated his daughters. Someone should've strung him up by the fingernails long ago.

"And then," Craig rushed on without even taking a breath, "there's the fact that I care a lot about what happens to Walsh Enterprises. Jolene is a hell of a lot better at running the business than Mark ever was. Together, she and I have probably added ten times more value to the outfit than he ever could've. I think the man might've been stealing from his own company. I could've killed him for that alone."

"Those are all good reasons for wanting someone dead but…" Jake eased around to study Craig's expression while the man bad-mouthed his old partner.

"I'm not even getting started yet." Craig lifted his eyes to Jake's and there was no mistaking the hatred. "Mark Walsh couldn't keep his dick in his pants. He humiliated his wife and kids. Stole the youth and joy from a couple of sweet young girls who didn't know any better. And he allowed a man to go to prison because of some perverted scheme he dreamed up for disappearing."

Craig finally wound down. "I could go on, but you get the picture. I'm glad he's dead. I only wish I *was* the one who ended his life."

"Yes, I can see that." Jake could see something else in Craig's eyes, too. An odd kind of weakness.

Up to that moment, he had thought of Craig as a

tough middle-aged man with fire in his belly. Passionate for his woman. Passionate about his business and for the kids he thought of as his own.

Now the spark was missing. A tiny flick of something painful in Craig's eyes said the man was suddenly feeling weak. Interesting, but none of Jake's business.

"Well, I'd better go see if Jolene needs my help," Craig told him. "It's been real nice talking to you, son. I hope you and Mary can make a go of things."

Jake had very little hope in that direction, but he lied again. "Thank you, sir. I hope so, too."

As he watched Craig leave, Jake mentally checked his name off his list of suspects. Not that Jake intended to stop looking into Craig's business records. But as far as murder was concerned, he didn't believe Craig Warner could have hurt anyone—not even a mosquito.

"I guess that takes care of everything," Mary told him an hour later. "All the guests have gone home. Did you have a chance to meet everyone?"

Jake could feel her withdrawal like a knife in the back. She hadn't said anything yet, but he had a feeling Mary would soon be telling him that she needed time to think.

He loved her enough to give her all the time in the world. But he didn't dare. Without protection, without truly understanding the threat, her life could be in grave danger. He had to find a way to convince her to come back to the house with him tonight. Not only had he made sure a state-of-the-art security alarm was installed in the house, but he'd also made arrangements with Jim to help keep an eye on them tonight. Mary was much safer there than she would be here at the farm.

Deep down, Jake had an ulterior motive for wanting her with him. Even beyond the sex. He planned on telling her the truth about himself first thing tomorrow morning when they could plan for her future safety. He had a feeling he knew how Mary would react to the news. But he kept on hoping he was wrong.

At least with the whole truth, she could make her own judgments about how best to stay safe. With help from the FBI. Perhaps she would ultimately decide to take a vacation until the investigation was over. He hoped she would. But it was killing him knowing they couldn't go together.

"Uh, Jake, I've been thinking," she began. "About tonight…"

No. He had to do something. He reached out, took her in his arms and planted a kiss on her mouth that nearly took him to his knees. God, they were good together.

After they both were thoroughly out of breath, he didn't want to let her go. But he finally needed to come up for air.

He quickly said, "Come home with me, Mary. Come home and let me show you how much I love you. I don't think I can adequately explain it in words. But…"

"You…love…me?" Her eyes were wide. Her lips wet and swollen by his kisses.

At this moment, he had never loved anyone more.

"Of course, I love you, my darling. Beyond words. Beyond reason. Please give me a chance to show you."

Confusion swam in her eyes and she bit her lip to make it stop trembling. "All right," she said shakily. "Then let's go on home."

Chapter 12

The professional assassin known as the Pro melded his body to the tree behind him. He was beginning to recognize every twig, branch and rock in these woods. Stationing himself here in the pines for most of the day, he'd watched the comings and goings at the target's fire-bombed house. Not one of the feds swarming the area had been any the wiser to his existence.

All it took to outsmart them was a little luck and a lot of persistence. It so happened that Honey Creek's only part-time plumber lived in the closest neighboring house to the target's. The plumber and his family had gone off to visit in-laws. But when the feds made their usual neighborhood check after the fire, they had not bothered to interview any of the townspeople about the plumber's current whereabouts. The Pro had simply become the plumber. He was even using the plumber's van as a temporary surveillance headquarters.

Watching this house was easy, and what he'd seen instructive. After the firemen left, a team of federal agents showed up to wire the house with alarms and put new security features in place. Meanwhile another unit cleaned up the mess left by the Pro's firebomb. He had catalogued it all from his safe perch.

He hadn't needed to go in search of his targets. He'd known by all the fuss that they were coming back here tonight.

Good thing, he thought as he remembered the last few bits of torn paper in his pocket. He'd received written confirmation that half the final payment for this job had already been wired to his bank account. When he was through here tonight and had received confirmation of the second payment, everything, including paper, phones and weapons, would go up in another puff of smoke. No traces would be left to incriminate either himself or his employer.

This job was fast coming to a close. His employer had at last okayed the kill. The one part of his job that the Pro enjoyed more than any other.

The Pro heard a twig snapping in the forest nearby and turned his head to the sound. Someone else was also sneaking through these woods tonight? But who would dare sneak around the house where a federal agent was staying? No one, with the possible exception of another fed stationed outside to safeguard the inhabitants.

The Pro smiled wryly to himself in the darkness. Oh, good. A new game. Or at least a slightly changed game. Cat and mouse.

Searching through the shadows with his night-vision

goggles, the Pro spotted his unwary competitor as the anonymous fed scoured the woods looking for anything out of place. But the hapless fellow was not about to spot the Pro in time to save himself. Nor the trap headed his way.

Tonight the rules of the game were all in the Pro's favor.

As they slipped into the house through the kitchen door, Mary and Jake could not seem to keep their hands off each other. Mary's heart was fairly bursting with love.

She had never felt this way about any other person. Not even close. Willing to give up anything if that was what he asked, Mary clung to Jake, nestling against his side as he set the new alarm system.

Jake kept one arm around her waist while he used the other to punch in the security code. "Hang on, love. We have all night."

That was what he'd said, but then he tilted his chin and placed a kiss against her temple. A kiss that was gentle, tender. But she felt the pull between them as strong as ever when he lingered, breathing in the scent of her shampoo.

She suppressed a chuckle of pleasure, knowing what was coming next. Longing for it. She was dying to show him how much she loved him.

Jake stopped in the kitchen only long enough to grab a couple of cold drinks and put together a platter of sandwiches her mother had supplied. "We're not making any trips downstairs this time. Tonight I'm keeping you in my bed."

Her whole body sank into his as arm in arm they

headed up the stairs, each carrying refreshments in one hand. Mary refused to look at the ugly, unpainted boards covering the burned-out shell of the family room. The two of them had made body-melting memories in that room and she hated knowing it would never look the same.

But just maybe, she thought brightly, they would have a chance to put it back together and make new memories. Wouldn't that be fun? Remodeling the house so it represented both of them?

Earlier Jake had hinted he had something important to tell her, but that he wanted to wait until tomorrow morning to talk. A secret thrill shot up her arms as she considered what he might say. Would he ask her to move in with him permanently? Or would he come right out and ask her to marry him? That was what two people who loved each other did, wasn't it?

Mary had a strong suspicion they would be talking about one of those things in the morning. In fact, as she'd packed a little bag to leave the farm tonight, she'd told her mother not to expect her back for at least a few days. Her mother apparently guessed the potential of the situation immediately, and Mary had spotted tears welling in Jolene's eyes. Her mother must've realized she was finally about to see her lonely little girl truly happy for the first time.

Mary couldn't wait for the future. Couldn't wait for tomorrow and all the rest of her tomorrows. Big changes in her life loomed directly ahead. Drawing in a breath, she tried to calm down as the excitement shimmered off her shoulders and bounced around the walls of their love nest.

This was going to be the best night of her entire life.

After they entered the master bedroom and set their burdens of food and drinks down on a side table, Mary immediately reached for the hem of her blouse. Ready to dispense with all her clothes so she could really get close to Jake, she was disappointed when he stayed her hands.

"Don't," he said softly. His gaze raked her body head to toe and fire landed everywhere he looked. "Let me do that for you."

Oh, yeah. The best night ever.

He slipped off his shoes, dumped the contents of his pockets on the dresser and reached for the buttons of his own shirt. But as he shrugged out of the sleeves, he drew in a breath and wrinkled his nose.

"Man, do I ever stink. Would you believe that after four or five showers today I still smell like smoke? And like sweat. Damn. Standing over a hot charcoal grill all night hasn't done a lot for my manly scent, has it?"

"I like your scent just fine." She reached for him but he backed away.

"Hold that thought. Give me a few minutes to clean up, love. I'll jump in the shower and…" He ran a flattened palm over his jaw. "Shave. And be back before you miss me."

"I miss you already."

Jake grinned and leaned in for a quick kiss. "Me, too. Don't move." Swinging around, he started for the bathroom before turning back. "And don't take anything else off. That's my job."

She laughed out loud this time and wrapped her arms around her middle, reveling in the warm love blanketing the room. What a difference a few weeks could make in someone's life. Not that long ago she'd been sure she would never find anyone to love. That she was destined to live as someone's daughter, sister and aunt but would never have a family of her own. She'd been absolutely convinced that the only families she would ever know were the ones found inside books.

But now look where she was. Completely in love and in her mind already building houses, marriages and maybe even children into a future so full of promise it was making her head swim.

Feeling light-headed, Mary plopped down on the bed and kicked off her shoes. Her whole body hummed in anticipation.

She listened to the water running in the bathroom and fidgeted for a moment. Wanting to join him in the shower, it was everything she could do to keep all her clothes on and stay seated on the bed. There would be time enough tonight for another shower or maybe two. Time enough to have tons of showers for the rest of their lives, in fact.

Trying to distract herself, Mary used her forefinger to push the change from Jake's pocket across the shiny flat surface of the nightstand. Quarters and dimes. She lined them up like a little row of tin soldiers.

Her gaze landed on his wallet next and she couldn't resist picking it up. Soft and supple, the dark red leather felt warm in her hand. And when she breathed in its smell, reminiscent of men's dens and lodges, the wallet seemed to come alive.

As she stroked along the stitched edges, she began to think about how a wallet contained a person's whole life story. She knew hers held identification, money to buy whatever she needed or wanted, and pictures of loved ones to remind her of who she was. A wallet could be considered a microcosm of someone's life.

Mary lifted her head when the shower stopped running in the bathroom. But then another faucet went on and she figured Jake was shaving. Maybe she could take a tiny peek inside his wallet before he finished and came back to bed.

What harm would it do? After their talk tomorrow morning, she would belong with him. The two of them would be a couple. They wouldn't keep any secrets from each other ever again.

Using just a fingernail, Mary flipped open the wallet. The first thing she saw was his driver's license. Jake Pierson. Age: 35. Height: six feet. Weight: 185. Eyes: blue. Hair: dark blond.

Staring down at his picture, Mary started to daydream the way she never had as a teen. Mary Pierson. Mrs. Jake Pierson. Mary Walsh Pierson. Wife. Mother. Lover.

Sighing, she flipped through the rest of the cards in his wallet. She found a credit card, social security card and a real estate license for the state of Montana. But no pictures.

Not one picture. She looked in the folding money section and found a few bills but nothing else. About to give up and put the wallet back down, she noticed the tiny edge of a paper sticking out from one side pocket.

Imagining it was some kind of receipt for his work, she slipped her fingers down into the pocket and rescued the folded paper. It turned out to be a piece of yellowed newspaper.

A newspaper clipping? For a man who refused to

carry around even one photo except on his driver's license, Jake had saved an old clipping? How strange.

Carefully, Mary unfolded the paper and smoothed it out on the top of the nightstand under the light. The headline read: Young Woman and Unborn Child Killed in Tragic Car Accident.

Mary quickly scanned the top of the page. The banner announcement came from the Santa Bertha, California, *Herald* and was datelined ten years ago last June. The first paragraph of the story recounted a horrific tale of a young pregnant woman struck in a head-on collision with an over-the-road truck not five miles from her own home.

With her hands shaking, Mary picked up the paper and held it closer to the light. A picture had been included at the bottom of the article. A smiling picture of a pretty blonde woman, wearing a wedding dress and standing beside her handsome new husband in his tuxedo.

No captions appeared under the picture, but Mary could not mistake the man's face. Even ten years younger, the man in a tuxedo had to be Jake.

She ran her finger down the article, searching for names. The first paragraph referred to the woman as Tina Summers. And then as Mrs. Jacob Summers further down in the article.

Oh, my God.

Jake had been married once. He'd lied to her.

And what was with the name? Summers? Had he changed his name? Was he hiding from something? Or someone?

What if he was one of those men who lived secret lives? With wives in two or three different states?

Her pulse rate kicked into high gear, and Mary's overactive imagination jumped to several different conclusions at the same time.

He could be a bigamist. He could be a fraud, wanting to marry her for her family's money. He could be wanted by the police. He could be a...murderer.

That last idea forced her to her feet. What was she doing here with a man she'd only met a few short weeks ago? All she knew about him for sure was that he was a liar. He could be anything.

Mary heard the water in the bathroom stop running. With her stomach in her throat, she couldn't catch her breath and her mind blanked. She had to get out of here.

Now.

Grabbing her purse, she tore open the bedroom door and banged down the hall in the dark toward the front stairs. She raced to leave the house before Jake could stop her.

Her heart pounded crazily inside her chest as she hit the top of the stairs.

"Mary?"

Oh, my God. Jake was out of the bathroom and had already discovered she was gone.

Mary picked up her speed and sprinted down the staircase, taking two stairs at a time. She had to get free to call for help.

Reaching out with both hands, she made a grab for the front-door handle. But when she tugged, nothing happened.

She remembered the new security measures Jake had mentioned. But what about emergencies?

Frantically, she worked on the door locks. Twisting and tugging.

"Mary? Where the hell…" He was at the top of the stairs!

At last, the handle turned and the door came free. But it opened with an alarm blast so loud the sound nearly knocked her down. The outside spotlights automatically came on and sirens screeched into the night as she dashed out the door.

"Damn it, Mary! Don't…"

Jake's words were lost in the chaos while she ran across the wide front porch. No. No. No. She couldn't let him catch her.

The same terrible truth kept repeating in her mind. She didn't even know his real name. Who was he really?

How could she have been this stupid?

Down the front steps she flew, checking over her shoulder to make sure he was not right behind her. What if… What if…

When she hit the ground, she headed down the sidewalk going toward the driveway. If she could make it out to the street, her cell phone should work and she could call for someone to come pick her up.

As she ran past the family room, the smell of charred wood reached her nose. She turned her head to look at the burned-out hulk of the room, but she wasn't about to slow down to look closer.

Mary let loose a loud scream as she tripped over something and took a header into a shrub.

What the heck could've been lying across the sidewalk in the middle of the night? No lights were on in the burned-out section of the house and it was blacker than pitch here beside it. Mary came up on her hands and knees and felt around in the dark, looking for her purse.

Her hand hit something solid. Big. Slightly warm.

Gingerly touching the object, Mary's wildest imagination raged free. She patted and brushed over the form until her hand hit something sticky. Pulling back, she shrieked again. Louder this time.

Even in the dark she could tell this object was a man's body. And she'd read enough murder mysteries to know the sticky substance had to be blood.

Panicked and nearing hysteria, Mary jumped to her feet. Purse or no purse, she was out of here.

But she was all turned around in the dark. Taking two big steps, she realized she was heading back toward the house. Twirling, she blindly dashed off in the opposite direction.

"That's far enough." Strong arms reached out and grabbed her by the shoulders.

But that wasn't Jake's voice. She had never heard this male voice before in her life. Big hands dug painfully into her shoulders and a whiskered jaw scraped her cheek.

"You may have to give it one more scream, girl," the man whispered in her ear. "Your lover has exactly two seconds to show up or it'll be too late to say goodbye."

What? What did he say?

Mary tried to twist out of his grip, but it was useless. Finally she kicked back at his shins and connected.

"Damn it, bitch."

Out of the total darkness came a swift blow to the side of her head. She screamed again.

"That's more like it. Call him to you so you can die together, you stupid whore."

At that moment, more yard lights came on and the entire area was lit up like a used-car lot.

"Jake! No! Stay back! He's going to…"

Another blow to the temple turned the bright lights off again for Mary—as everything in her world went completely black.

Chapter 13

When he heard the first scream, a burst of adrenaline drove Jake down the front stairs running after Mary. But after hearing her scream for the second time, a shot of good sense and extreme caution kept him from chasing her outside.

One scream from her could've meant surprise at finding Jim outside guarding the house. But a second scream worried Jake and made him stop long enough to think. He swung around in mid-stride and headed into the kitchen to retrieve his weapon, thanking God that he'd thought to pull on his jeans before dashing from the bathroom.

By the time he had the gun in hand and sprinted out through the kitchen door and past the gate, the shrieking alarm had shut off by itself. Probably on a timer. More concerned than ever in the silence, Jake rounded the corner of the house. He stopped long enough to flip on a second set of outside floodlights.

Moving on, Jake experienced a sudden flood of fear and panic, too reminiscent of long ago. Ten excruciating long years ago to be exact. The woman he'd loved then was struck down in a startling flash of pain and blood. Killed too young—due to his foolish actions. He'd been young and full of himself, and the person he'd loved died because he was thoughtless and selfish.

Afterward, Jake had been convinced that he would never be capable of loving again. Once was all he got in his lifetime. He'd devoted his life to his work. And in all the years since, no one else had moved him the way his wife had. No one else had managed to open him up. No one else ever bothered to dig under his pain.

Not until now. Not until Mary.

With yet another scream from her, Jake came to his senses, jogging in place on the pine needle–covered sidewalk. The situation must be worse than he'd imagined. She had to be in trouble. Crouching low, he peered through the charred remnants of the family room, hoping to spy movement.

What he saw at the front of the house sent a zing of dread through his veins. Through the stealthy shadows, a bulky figure of a man raised one arm and struck Mary in the temple with what seemed to be a Ruger .44. A frigging big weapon, outfitted with a heavy crimson trace. Mary's knees gave out under the blow and her attacker grabbed her around the waist, pulling her closer to his body in order to keep her upright.

Jake's hands fisted. Fear and fury blinded him for the moment. But after gulping in air, he soon channeled the rage, drawing on his training. He forced any unprofessional thoughts of Mary as the woman he loved into a dark recess of his mind.

Tactics. Remember the breathing. Assess all the possibilities.

While Jake's brain tried to process the scene, their assailant seemed to be assessing possibilities, too. With Mary under one arm, the man backed up to the blackened ruins of the family room—directly in front of Jake's position. Meanwhile, the guy's gun arm arched out, sighting a point of red laser light to both the right and the left.

The gunman must've been hoping for a head-on confrontation. But since Jake had not raced right into his trap after Mary's scream, the assailant was finding his own caution.

An outright confrontation would get both Jake and Mary killed without a fight. And Jake didn't have a clean shot. Not without taking far too great a chance on hitting Mary. An alternative had to be found—and quickly. The assailant might be a pro, but he had misjudged both Jake's determination and his skill.

Jake carefully began picking his way through the part of charred family room that wasn't covered by boards and headed straight for the target. The only chance of surprise in this situation was to sneak between the downed timbers and charcoaled floorboards without making any sound and attack the man from behind. Jake had spent all afternoon in these ruins and figured he could maneuver here with his eyes closed.

Sliding sideways through the blackened timbers, Jake floated along like a ghost shadow. He kept his peripheral vision trained on the target, hoping to do nothing that might alert the assailant to the threat sneaking up behind his back.

As he closed in, Jake heard Mary moaning. Then she moved. Infinitesimally at first, but soon she was squirming in her attacker's grip.

Grateful for small but significant favors, Jake breathed more evenly. Obviously, her injuries were not immediately life-threatening. She was alive. And—she was becoming a major distraction to their assailant at the best moment possible.

Come on. Easy now. Don't anyone make any sudden moves. Let me get a little closer.

Two more steps.

"Show yourself, Pierson! Your woman needs you. Come out and we'll talk." The man jammed his weapon to Mary's temple.

The screech of sirens ringing in the distance suddenly captured the assailant's attention. For only an instant. The security alarm had apparently done its work, summoning help to the fray.

With her assailant's momentary distraction, Mary took the opportunity and planted her feet, spinning free of his grip. The assailant whipped his gun around, putting her directly in his sights.

Jake didn't hesitate. He launched his body through the last three feet of burned-out building, taking the other man to the ground right at the exact moment the weapon fired.

Mary. Jake wanted to check on her welfare, but could not lose his focus. Not yet.

He pinned the assailant's gun hand. The man arched his body, trying to buck Jake off. But Jake hung on, slamming the hand with the weapon into the sidewalk. Once. And again. Over and over until the .44 flew free.

Then Jake's hands went to the man's throat. He squeezed, putting pressure against the gunman's windpipe. Deep down Jake wanted to kill the bastard for hurting Mary. It was all he could do not to squeeze too hard.

The assailant panicked, twisting and kicking until Jake's grip loosened. Out of nowhere, the son of a bitch freed a hand and caught him in the chin with an uppercut. But Jake wasn't about to let the asshole squirm totally free. He pummeled him—in the nose and in the gut.

"Stop! Or…or I'll shoot." Mary stood about ten feet away with her attacker's bulky weapon in both her hands. "Get up."

The assailant stopped fighting immediately. Jake jumped to his feet, dragging the man up with him.

"You won't shoot me," the assailant told Mary with a sneer. "You don't have it in you, librarian."

Jake feared the SOB was probably right, but he wouldn't show any weakness or lack of faith in the woman he loved. Sirens, still screaming through the chilled night air, were coming closer. All he and Mary needed were a few more minutes and their stand-off would be over.

"Who are you and why have you been stalking us? Why try to kill us?" Jake demanded.

Needing a momentary distraction, Jake tried to tempt their assailant into talking instead of acting in panic. Jake also wanted a reason. A name behind the attacks.

Their assailant shrugged, then grinned. "All in a day's work, pal."

In a surprise move, the man ripped his arms free of Jake's grip and spun, heading straight for Mary. She raised the heavy weapon in both hands and took aim. Her whole body shook so badly that Jake worried she might shoot him instead.

As the assailant overtook her, she managed to discharge the gun. But her shot went wild.

However, Jake's shot did not. Their assailant was dead before he ever hit the ground.

It was over that fast.

"Jake! Are you okay?" Mary flew at him, landing against his chest and throwing her arms around his neck. She covered his face in kisses.

He eased both his own weapon and Mary's to the ground and then closed his arms around her, reveling in the feel of her warm body. She was alive and breathing. And Jake felt nearly faint with relief.

Mary eased back in his arms and gazed into his eyes. "Was it my shot that killed him? I was so afraid for you."

Spectacular. "No, my love. You're no killer. But without your actions, we might not have made it."

Jake would never love her any more than he did right this minute. The woman was beyond strong, both emotionally and physically. It thrilled him to see the way she'd been fierce in her determination both to live and to save his life. Determined, because she still had no idea about his lies.

For the moment.

A little later, Jake sat back on his heels beside the body of his partner with memories flooding his mind.

Memories of missions won and lost. Of a decade of years, some with near misses and many with clear victories. Years of being there to watch each other's back and to give assistance when things got rough.

Scraping a hand across his eyes, Jake murmured, "How could this happen? You…taking one for me? If anyone should've died here, partner, it should've been me. I'm a miserable nothing and you had it all. This was my show. My…mistake."

Jake heard heavy footsteps behind his back, but he didn't move. What for?

"I just got off the phone with your boss, Pierson." The voice belonged to the sheriff. "SAC Benton is en route. Should be here within an hour and a half. He'll be bringing a forensics team with him but he wants us to secure the scene and do our best to keep a lid on things."

Jake didn't turn. His eyes weren't focusing and his brain wasn't fully engaged.

"Uh…" Wes cleared his throat. "He also asked me to take charge of your weapons. Only for the time being, you understand."

Jake waved a hand toward the two weapons, lying not far away on the ground. "One is my personal weapon. The other belongs to the unsub. There's also my 10 mm service pistol in a duffel in the master bedroom closet."

He wasn't ready to mention the Glock 9 mm hidden in the SUV. That one would stay hidden for a while.

"Jake…" Wes put a hand on his shoulder. "The county coroner is on his way out to make the pronouncements. Let me cover Jim's body until he arrives. He was my friend from our SEAL days, too, remember."

Jake got to his feet, closed his eyes for an instant then turned to face the sheriff. "Do it."

After Wes spread a Mylar blanket over his partner's body, Jake finally felt able to take his first deep breath since the shooting. "How's Mary?"

"She's with the paramedic. Looks and sounds a little shaky to me, but a lot calmer than most civilians after going through what she did. I can hardly believe Mary actually took a shot at the assailant and then witnessed him die. Most women would be hysterical."

"I know. But Mary's pretty tough." Somehow Jake wasn't the least surprised by the revelation.

"Melissa doesn't believe Mary's in shock, but she wants to take her to the Bozeman hospital for an evaluation and a CT scan. She says Mary's got a hell of a goose egg on her head."

Jake nodded. "Bozeman would be good. Anywhere out of Honey Creek. When is she going?"

"Mary claims she won't leave until she talks to you."

Ah, hell. Jake fisted his hands but knew it was time to man up. Mary deserved answers.

"And Melissa is insisting," Wes went on, "that your cuts and scrapes need to be cleaned and your feet checked before she's free to take Mary anywhere."

"My feet?" Jake looked down and realized for the first time that he was barefoot. "I'm fine. Tell the paramedic not to concern herself."

Wes didn't reply but turned and made his way over to the body of the unsub. "This bastard had been stalking you and Mary."

"I know. That's why I asked Jim to keep an eye on us from outside the alarm perimeter tonight."

Wes screwed up his mouth and nodded before bending to inspect the attacker's corpse. "We found a tree perch in the woods that the stalker must've been using," he said over his shoulder. "And my men located a sniper rifle that was probably the one that took out your partner."

Jake walked over to where Wes was bending over to pat down the unsub. He stood beside the sheriff, gazing down at the man he'd killed and feeling nothing. Absolutely nothing.

Wes had another question for him. "You have any idea why this character would've suddenly decided to kill you instead of sticking with the games he'd been playing?" Wes was gingerly checking the dead man's pockets.

"The bastard was a pro. He was only taking orders." And maybe that was why Jake didn't harbor any guilt for killing the man. He felt as if he'd stopped a robot, a machine aimed at hurting Mary.

Wes turned his head to look up at Jake. "Orders from whom?"

"Exactly. But it's not my investigation. Not anymore."

"Yeah?" Wes's eyes narrowed and he went back to checking the unsub's body. "Well, I've got two more dead bodies on my hands. I know the Bureau will want to investigate the death of one of their own, but I don't much like the idea of having a murder spree in my town. Especially not one involving the murder of a friend."

Wes pulled a few tiny slips of paper from the dead man's pants pocket. "What have we here?" He removed his flashlight from its place at his belt and studied the papers in brighter lighting.

After a moment Wes said, "It looks like part of an execution order—on you. Written by hand on some pretty fancy-looking stationary." Wes tried to piece together two of the tiny scraps of paper. "But why would anyone keep incriminating evidence like this on their person?"

Jake shrugged. "Insurance, maybe. You know, in case he was caught and needed to make a deal."

"Maybe. But the signature is missing. Almost everything needed to identify the writer is missing, actually."

"Have SAC Benton's team do a full forensic workup and then copy you the results."

Wes nodded, but folded the smallest scrap of paper and placed it in his breast pocket. "I'll turn it over. But this expensive stationary is rather rare for our part of the country. I have an idea or two that need following up."

Jake nodded, too. He understood taking tiny shortcuts in order to stay a step ahead of an investigation. And in this case, nothing major would be lost by the sheriff holding on to a nonessential part of the evidence.

Jake didn't consider falling in love a shortcut—not exactly. But everything major in his world had been lost due to his stepping away from procedure. And the idea was killing him.

"I'm going over to talk to Mary." Jake turned, started to walk away from Wes but twisted around to add, "Can one of your guys bring me a pair of boots from upstairs?"

Wes nodded and Jake kept walking. It felt as if he was marching straight into the depths of hell—to the one thing he had been dreading the most.

But it had to be done. His investigation had put Mary in danger and she needed to accept close personal protection from now on, with or without him around, and it was up to Jake to see that she understood why.

"But I don't understand what happened here." Mary could hear her tone of voice rising a couple of octaves but it was beyond her to stop. "No one will tell me anything. Who was that man and why did he try to kill us?"

Her hands had stopped shaking, but her head was starting to pound. Still, she refused to leave or lie down or take any medication until she talked to Jake.

Jake turned to Melissa, who had finished dabbing antiseptic to the cuts on his hands and face. "Can you give us a few moments?" he asked her.

"Sure. I'll go notify the Bozeman hospital we're coming in." She turned to study Mary for a second. "Be back in a few."

Jake stood, leaving Mary the only one still sitting on the back of the paramedic's truck. He watched Melissa walk away, then he turned to Mary and took her by the hand.

"This is all my fault. But I…but I…" He hung his head and dropped her hand.

"Jake, what is it? Why would any of this be your fault? You saved us." It was then she noticed the blood spattered all over his clothing. Suddenly chilled, she rubbed up and down her arms trying to find warmth.

He looked her straight in the eye and stopped hedging. "I've been lying to you. Right from the start. I'm sorry. I should've told you what was going on—who I really am—long ago. But I knew if I did you wouldn't…you would…"

"Lying?" The word filled her mind with the terrible images that she had thought she'd conquered. "About what? About being in love with me? About being married?" She wasn't sure she could stand to hear what he had to say.

Her forehead broke out in a cold sweat.

"I do love you." The plea in his voice for her to understand almost cut through the pain in her heart. Almost.

"But that's about the only thing that wasn't a lie. I'm an undercover agent for the FBI, Mary. My partner and I have been working a covert operation on a Racketeer Influenced and Corrupt Organizations case. We're here trying to open up an international money-laundering scheme—originating in Honey Creek."

"What?" Confused, Mary put a hand to her temple, wanting to make the throbbing in her head subside. "You're not in real estate?"

He kept his eyes trained on her face, watching her closely. "I'm an FBI special agent. My partner Jim…" Jake's face blanched when he mentioned his partner's name.

Sudden images of the two men lying on the ground, bloody and not breathing, caused Mary's stomach to roll. Oh, God, she was going to be sick.

"Jim is the man you found. The dead man you tripped over." Jake's eyes closed for an instant before he began again. "It all started when your father contacted one of our foreign offices while he was in Costa Rica. He wanted to…"

"My father? Costa Rica? What on earth are you saying?"

Mary felt light-headed. And cold. She wanted to lie down. She wanted to run away and hide. Hide from the death. Hide from the blood. Hide from the truth.

None of this conversation made sense and the only subjects that interested her right now were how Jake was handling the shooting and what he wanted to say. But she could feel him pulling away from her.

Was her connection with Jake going to be yet one more thing her father had destroyed in her life?

Chapter 14

"It's a long story and I don't have time right now to tell you everything." Jake's face took on a slightly green cast as if he felt sick, too. "Only that your father had been living in Costa Rica. But he wanted to come back to the States. He contacted the U.S. State Department who put him in touch with the Bureau, and they made him a deal."

Jake stopped speaking for a moment and picked up her hands. "You're cold." His eyes were full of concern… and something else she couldn't name.

But concern wasn't what she wanted from him. She pulled away and folded her hands in her lap. "I'm okay. Go on."

"Mark Walsh was supposed to provide us with the details of an international money-laundering operation, on the condition that the State Department would allow him back into the country and grant him immunity from prosecution."

"Let me get this straight. You're here because you were supposed to get information from my father?" Mary's head whirled in a state of confusion. This wasn't what she'd expected to hear.

Jake blinked, reaching for her again. Then he suddenly dropped his hands back to his sides. "I was supposed to interview him here in Honey Creek and follow up on his information. His body was found the day before our meeting was to take place."

Mary wrapped her arms around her waist, growing colder. "Okay. Okay. You were undercover. But…" She looked up at his beloved face. "Why me? Why did you make…friends…with me? To get information? But I don't know anything. I didn't even know my father was still alive."

The ache in her chest was becoming much worse than the ache in her head. She rubbed over it with one palm.

Jake's face contorted, as though he, too, felt great pain. "I needed an intro to the community. Someone who was familiar with the Walsh family and could get me inside. That was you."

Oh, God. Mary wanted to run, but Jake was standing close. Too close. She couldn't breathe.

"Then everything you said—all the things you told me were lies?"

"Listen to me," he said, his voice hoarse and breathless. "The stories about my past were true—most of them. I wanted to tell you the rest. The complete truth. But when I realized you weren't involved in anything illegal, it was too late. By then I knew you would never tolerate a liar."

In a much quieter voice, Jake added, "And by then I didn't want to lose you. I was already in too deep."

Sudden, intense anger snapped up and out of her mouth without warning. "You bastard! You used me. I almost died a couple of times and I would've never known why."

"I planned on telling you. First thing in the morning. Remember that I had something to say?"

"You were planning on telling me…about this? About your mission?" A red rage blinded her, making her say things before she thought them through. "I hate you. Go away."

"There's something else we have to discuss first. I need a few more minutes."

She jumped up, raised her arm and smacked him hard across the cheek. Damn. Mary had never hit anyone before in her life and the minute she had, she felt completely devastated.

Jake never flinched. He just stood there looking as though he deserved everything she could do to him.

Pulling the yellowed newspaper clipping from her pocket, she confronted him with it—swiping it under his nose. "I don't want to hear anything you have to say. Not unless it's about your dead wife. You remember, the one you never had?"

"You found that. You went snooping in my wallet?" Jake rubbed a hand over his jaw. "I shouldn't have been carrying that clipping. It was my first breach of protocol. I have never done anything this dangerous to the mission before in my entire career."

Mary threw it at him and turned away. "Never mind.

I won't believe anything you have to say, anyway. You're worse than my father ever was."

"Wait." Jake put a hand on her shoulder, his touch so light and gentle it nearly brought her to tears.

She stopped, but had to wage a battle with herself not to turn into his arms.

"Mary, you may hate me. I don't blame you. But I didn't lie about loving you. Never doubt that. You are a very special woman. After my wife died, I was positive there couldn't be anyone else for me. Not ever.

"But then I met you and everything changed. You touched me. Worked your way into my heart without me noticing until it was too late. Now I would gladly give up everything—my job and my whole life—for your sake. I would take a bullet for you without giving it a second thought."

Mary heard the tremor in his voice but refused to turn around.

"But I know you won't let me give you what you need most right now. You need protection, my love, twenty-four seven. Whoever hired our stalker may try again. Wes and the Bureau will do everything in their power to get the word out that you don't know anything. That there's no reason to come after you. But still…"

She turned and lifted her chin. "I don't need anything."

"Yes, I'm afraid you do. You need a guard. At least for a while. And the Bureau will insist you take their help."

"But not help from you." She wanted him gone. Out of her sight. She had to be alone to scream and cry out her pain.

"Not if you don't want me."

"I don't want you. I don't love you. I've never loved you and I don't believe anything you have to say."

Tears threatened to leak from the corners of her eyes and make a liar out of her. She bit her tongue to force them back inside. "Just leave me alone, Jake. I'm done. I've had all the lies from you I can stand.

"I thought I knew you," she added sadly. "But I was wrong. You are exactly like my father. The world's biggest liar. I never want to see you again. Stay away from me."

As dawn broke over Honey Creek, the lavender dew covered both sidewalks and pines. Jake was impervious to the beauty around him while he sat quietly on the front steps of the rental house. Resting his chin on his fists, he waited for his boss to finish up on the SAT phone.

An image of Mary, looking fragile and broken as he'd trampled her dreams, kept intruding upon his thoughts. She hadn't been aware of his pain, but every word she'd uttered in response to his *truths* would forever be engraved in his memory. Each syllable, each dagger of her rage, had sliced him into raw pieces, until at the end of her tirade, he was sure the jigsaw puzzle that used to be Jake Pierson would never be solved again.

He'd been concerned about her going into shock. She'd exhibited all the signs. Seeing a man shot right in front of her eyes and almost dying herself must have affected her more deeply than she'd let on. So he had let her rant.

He'd deserved her rage. He deserved much worse. If he could take back everything that had happened between them he would—except for falling in love with her. Loving her was the only spark of decent behavior he had exhibited through his entire mission.

He was grateful to Melissa for taking Mary to the Bozeman hospital several hours ago. Wes had just received word that, though she was not in immediate danger, the doctors wanted to keep Mary there under observation until tomorrow.

Not a bad thing. Mary would be safe in Bozeman. Wes said he would leave men to guard her while she was in the hospital.

Jake took the sheriff's word as gospel. He had all the respect in the world for Wes. At odd moments in the past few hours, the two of them had silently bonded over the loss of their friend Jim. His partner's death was a shared link between them—a devastating and excruciating tie.

Now Jake sat waiting to talk to his boss about what would happen to Mary after she was released from the hospital. The Bureau needed a fresh plan for her as well as for the rest of the mission, but Jake's brain was too fried to be of much help in devising any schemes for the future. He could barely decide what to do for the rest of the day.

Looking up through the tidy chaos that arose around the FBI's team of forensic investigators, Jake saw SAC Gerald Benton heading in his direction.

"You sure you don't need medical attention?" the SAC asked when he came close.

Ripping off the bandage Jake had allowed the paramedic to tape over one of his cuts last night, he found no fresh blood. "All healed." At least physically.

"I don't think you've had a chance to meet the special agent who's due to arrive momentarily, Pierson. He's newly assigned to the investigation here in Honey Creek. You two will need to spend time together."

"Ah… About that…"

SAC Benton waved away any objections. "I know. You're off the mission. But the information you've already collected will be invaluable. After your critical-incident debriefing, I expect you to give the new man all the time he needs."

Jake shook his head slowly. "I'll write a wrap-up report. Then I'm done. You can have my badge and gun. America will have to get by rounding up bad guys without me. I quit."

His boss regarded him carefully then sat down on the step beside him. "The FBI lost a good man when they lost Jim Willis. And you lost one hell of a partner. But Jim wouldn't want you to make any hasty decisions. You're a damned good undercover operative. Take some time off. You've earned it. Don't throw away a stellar career."

A stellar career? Not so much. A career full of psychotic disassociation was more like it. Years of dropping out of your own personality in order to become someone else wasn't exactly Jake's idea of the most heroic choice in occupations.

"My decision isn't hasty, Benton. I've been thinking about quitting for several years. For Jim's sake, I only wish I had gotten out before it was too late."

"You have to take a mandatory psych eval after your debriefing on the shooting. Talk to the psychologists about your partner's death. Give them and yourself time."

Jake stared at the ground, trying to dredge up some loyalty to the Bureau or some emotion over having had to kill a man. But all he felt was empty. His partner was gone. The love of his life had walked away for good. Any residual feeling about the job couldn't compete.

"I don't need therapy. Sorry, Benton. I'm just finished with the FBI for good."

SAC Benton threw up his hands and walked away, muttering something else about more time. But within fifteen minutes his boss was back with the new special agent assigned to the Honey Creek case.

"Pierson, this is Ethan Ross. Talk to him."

Jake looked up and nodded, but he didn't bother to stand or shake hands. It wasn't his fight anymore.

"I'm sorry about your partner, Special Agent Pierson."

"Me, too." Jake finally came to his feet. "There isn't much I can tell you about Honey Creek or the people here that you can't read in my reports, Ross. It's a nice little town for the most part."

"I've been going over the transcripts of that computer tap you managed at Walsh Enterprises," Special Agent Ross told him. "Nice work, but I'm afraid there's nothing there to help the investigation. We did get a lucky break in the case, though."

"Yeah?" Jake didn't care. He was having trouble caring about anything but Mary's safety.

"Damned right." Agent Ross nodded and went on with his explanation. "There's suddenly no real need to replace you with an undercover operative in Honey Creek. We've come up with a new informant. A volunteer. Someone with better access than you had. This person is already a part of the community."

Confused, Jake shook his head in denial. "Nearly everyone in this town is a suspect—if not for our RICO

investigation then in one of the murder investigations."
He searched through his mental notes for who the
volunteer informant might be but came up empty.

"Our new informant has already been vetted and
is definitely not under suspicion." Ross spoke with a
deliberate but friendly air, almost as if this investigation
was just a walk in the park. "Having someone like this
informant on our team will be exactly what we need to
break the case."

"Good for you." But Jake didn't give a damn.

Sure, he wanted a name for the person who'd put out
the order for his execution—the name of the unsub's
boss. But he wanted that info only in order to be assured
of Mary's safety. Jake had a gut feeling Wes's murder
investigations might turn up persons of interest a hell
of a lot faster than the Bureau's RICO investigation
would.

Jake agreed to write up his report as fast as possible
and send it on to Special Agent Ross within the next
twenty-four hours—along with his formal resignation. He
couldn't wait to wash his hands of this investigation—or
of the entire FBI for that matter. They didn't interest
him.

Nothing did. Not without Mary.

When he finally had the time to do a serious inventory
of what mattered to him now, Jake wasn't sure he could
find anything to take her place. Maybe he never would.
At the moment, the only spark of interest he could find
buried under all his emotional and mental baggage was
a nagging worry about Mary's safety.

He clung to the tiny but real emotion like a lifeline,
and went off to plead with SAC Benton for long-term
protection for her.

* * *

"You did what?" Wes was staring at him as though he'd announced he was taking up cannibalism.

"I quit the Bureau. Once I debrief, go through the regular internal investigation on the clean shooting and write my report, I'm gone."

The forensics team had finished up hours ago. The bodies had been removed. And SAC Benton and Special Agent Ross had taken off for the field office. A special cleanup crew would be sent in to complete the rebuilding on the leased house. Then it would be returned to its out-of-state owner's possession. Everything else was supposed to go back to normal in and around Honey Creek, allowing the FBI's investigation to continue unimpeded.

But Jake was having trouble moving away from this spot, these woods, and vaguely understood he couldn't seem to find much enthusiasm for leaving town.

"I see," Wes said quietly. "What do you plan on doing next?"

Jake shrugged a shoulder and looked toward the woods, at the pines and firs that were beginning to get under his skin. He breathed in the heady scent of sage and that woodsy musk peculiar to this valley and regretted having to leave at all. On the other hand, everything here reminded him too much of Mary. Was too intimately connected to her in his mind.

"No clue yet," he finally replied. "The only thing I seem to care about is making sure Mary stays safe."

Wes scowled. "I've already said I would see to that. She's one of mine. As long as she's in this town, she will be safe. No need for you to concern yourself over her."

Shoving his hands in his pockets, Jake leaned back on his heels and lowered his voice. "Mary is my only concern."

"Ah… I get it. Have you told her that? Does she know?"

"I'm not sure what she knows. She was pretty hot when she left. Said she never wants to hear from me again."

"Give her some time. There's too many new concepts for her to absorb them all at once." Wes folded his arms and shifted his stance. "You have a hometown somewhere with people anxious for you to come home?"

"No place…no people at all."

"How about money? Will you need to move fast to find a job to pay the bills?"

Jake shook his head. "Undercover work pays fairly well and I haven't had much in the way of a real life for years. Don't own anything and don't owe anyone. I'll have enough saved up along with enough back pay to get by for quite a while."

"Hmm. Well, I may have an idea or two for you when you're ready to hear about them."

"I'm not looking for a deputy sheriff's job, pal. Law enforcement has lost all its appeal. Along with everything else."

Wes's smile crinkled the corners of his eyes as he tilted his chin in thought. "Didn't I hear you claim a second ago that there was at least one thing you still cared about?"

"Mary's safety."

"Right." Wes gave him a friendly punch in the

shoulder. "Then let's go find us a cup of coffee and toss around a few ideas."

Someone was following her. Mary's heart pounded out a staccato rhythm. Oh, lordy, not again.

Racing her car down the back roads, she headed toward the farm. Why now? She hadn't even had a chance to go home since the shooting. Who would still want to cause her harm?

Suddenly it occurred to her that she couldn't lead whoever it was straight to her family. Slowing, she decided to face the danger head-on. But when she stopped the car and turned around to look, no one was there.

Exhaling, she waited for her pulse to calm. She wondered if the person following her might have been one of the sheriff's men. When Wes had come to check on her at the Bozeman hospital several days ago, he'd told her that he planned on having someone keep an eye on her when she got back to Honey Creek.

She'd almost forgotten because she hadn't come right home after being released from the hospital. The FBI had wanted her to come in to their field office in Bozeman for an interview and that had taken a couple of days. But staying off the farm, away from her family and Honey Creek, hadn't been any imposition.

Mary had needed those hours and days to think—to cry—and to let her body heal. The bruises were almost gone, but the clear thinking and the crying seemed only to be beginning. She'd been caught up in a kind of dreamland ever since the first instant she'd seen Jake. And coming down to earth was a big jolt of reality.

A reality that seemed to come with an ocean of tears.

The *affair,* for lack of a better word, with Jake *had* changed her. Changed her in many different ways. Her life would never be quite the same again.

Finally navigating up the driveway to the farm, Mary swore her new life would begin as soon as possible. Stopping the car in front of the farmhouse, she turned off her engine but didn't make a move to get out. She sat motionless, gazing out the windshield at the familiar surroundings.

She had grown up in this house. But it did not hold happy memories for her.

She had begun her journey to a new life in this house. But her journey would not be finished here.

This place was no longer hers. She'd changed and didn't feel at home here. She didn't feel at home anywhere.

She was lost. Completely rudderless with no one to talk to. Her friends and her family cared, but all had their own lives. None of them knew what she'd been through.

Oh, man, how Mary wished she and Jake could've remained on friendly terms. She could use a real friend about now.

Chapter 15

With her emotions raging, Mary eased out from the car and headed inside to find her mother. She needed to tell Jolene of her many life-changing decisions.

"There you are." Jolene came toward her daughter as soon as she walked through the front door. "I wish you would've let me pick you up and drive you home. I've been worried about you since you called."

"I'm fine, Mother." Four solid days of crying had left her red-eyed and weak, but Mary straightened her shoulders and faced her mother.

"Good. Where have you been anyway? It's so unlike you to just disappear with only a phone call. Were you with Jake? There's been a few rumors around town about strange things going on out at his house."

At the mention of his name, Mary's heart began to pound. Her palms began to sweat and the tears backed up in her eyes and throat yet again. But the FBI had made it clear she could not tell anyone what had taken place at Jake's. Or who Jake was under his guise as a real estate agent. Or what had happened to her. To them.

She couldn't even tell her family. Especially not her family.

And she did not dare allow herself to dwell on how much her heart still hurt without him—or her mother might see the truth too easily.

So Mary opened her mouth and for the first time in her life told her mother a deliberate lie. "You probably know about the little fire in one of the rooms of Jake's house. It wasn't anything major. The main thing is that Jake and I broke up. I needed a few days by myself to think. No big deal."

"Oh, honey, I'm sorry. I liked Jake. Are you okay? You've never gone off by yourself like that before."

Man, she hated lying to her mother, but she couldn't dwell on it because the time had come to share more important news.

She exhaled and said, "Mom, I'm moving out. I need to find a place of my own."

Instead of looking unhappy or confused, her mother nodded. "I agree. You need a new start, and I would love to help you find a place if you'd like. I know I haven't always been there for you like a mother should. I was so busy with the business and with making sure your father had everything he needed that I..." Jolene stopped talking and her eyes widened. "You're not planning on leaving Honey Creek, are you?"

"No, of course not. Honey Creek is my home." Not that the town had done such great things for her in the past. "I have family and friends here and I don't want to leave them behind. Besides, I can't think of anyplace else that is half as beautiful. I love this part of the country. Where else would I go?"

Jolene gave her a quick hug. "Good. I don't want to lose you before we can actually find time for a real relationship."

"It's okay, Mom. I know you're in love with Craig and your life is terribly busy. But I'll be around. We'll make time for each other from now on. Uh, look, I'm going to be packing up while I try to find a new place."

Then Mary thought of something else. "I need to run into town and turn in my final resignation before I do anything else. I've decided I can't continue working at the library."

"No?" Her mother didn't seem surprised at the news. "But what will you do? Do you want to come to work for Walsh Enterprises? We'd love to have you."

The idea was preposterous, but her mother was being thoughtful and that made Mary actually smile for the first time in days. "I don't know what I want to do exactly. But I can't work for Walsh Enterprises. There's too many unhappy memories there. I've been giving some thought to starting my own business."

"I've always believed you'd be great as a business owner, sweetheart. Like all the rest of us in the family. It's in the blood. But what kind of business?"

Mary shrugged and tilted her head, thinking. "That's the problem. I'm not sure. At first I thought maybe a bookstore, but there's not enough traffic for even a small bookstore in Honey Creek."

Jolene patted her on the shoulder. "Something will come to you. Don't worry. You're a bright young woman. I know you'll find the right thing."

Mary gave her mother a soft nod, but inside she wished she had the same confidence. She'd been so sure she had found the right thing with Jake. And look how well that had turned out.

Mary dabbed at her eyes as she walked out of the library's wide front doors and headed down the steps. She could hardly believe that after all these years she would never again have to come to work at the library. The idea was a little scary but thrilling at the same time.

She just wished Jake was here. She wanted to talk and share her feelings.

Not paying any attention to where she was going, Mary bumped headlong into two women coming up the stairs. "Oh, excuse me."

When she looked up, she realized it wasn't two women at all, but one woman in her late thirties or early forties and a teenager who was her spitting image.

Both had black hair and pretty blue eyes. Mary was taken by how nice they looked together, like a cozy family unit. She stood there gawking.

"I'd bet you're Mary Walsh," the woman said after she smoothed out a wrinkle in her dress. "You look a lot like your mother with all that red hair and those lovely amber eyes. I'm Lily Masterson, the new head librarian. And this is my daughter May."

Mary nodded and found her smile, the disguise she sometimes used in an effort to keep from being exposed. "You two are the ones that look alike. No one would ever miss guessing you're related."

"That's a wonderful compliment. For both of us.

Thank you." Lily laughed, the sound so pleasant that Mary's spirit felt a bit lighter.

"I vaguely remember you as a rather…uh…gawky teenager when I left town fifteen years ago." Lily seemed in no hurry to go inside. "You've changed since then. You're a beautiful woman, Mary. I was sorry to hear we won't be working together."

Mary managed another tentative smile. Then she suddenly remembered the many rumors that spread around town about Lily Masterson years ago, and she couldn't help but steal a quick glance at May. The young teenager was adorable, with her alabaster skin and dimpled smile. But Mary was positive she could not be related to the Walsh family. No possible way. She didn't look like any of them.

A secret pregnancy had been the rampant rumor of the day about Lily, of course. Supposedly, wild-child Lily had been having an affair with Mark Walsh before he'd disappeared.

Now Mary came to the conclusion that those rumors had to have been bogus. In fact, she was having some trouble with the whole concept of Lily as being wild at all. The librarian looked very much like a professional career woman and single mother. Someone that Mary would like to know.

Young May grinned over at her. "Mom says you've worked at the library for a number of years. What are you going to do now?"

"May," Lily scolded. "That's rude. We don't know…"

"No, it's okay." Mary's smile was completely genuine this time. "I'm not sure what I want to do. I have a lot of plans whirling in my head, but first I need to find a new place to live."

"Mom and I are living with my grandfather. He's getting older and doesn't feel well."

"I'm sorry to hear that. But it's nice that you can all be together."

May looked at her through thoughtful eyes that seemed older than her years. "Don't you have family here you can live with?"

"May…" Lily's face flushed as she glared at her daughter.

But Mary only chuckled and said, "I've been living with my mother, but I think it's time I found my own place. I'm all grown up now."

"Well, if I was old enough to go out on my own I would find me a big old house either in the woods or in the mountains. Anyplace outside of this town would be awesome. The town itself isn't much."

An idea sneaked up on Mary, jolting her in the head without warning. She loved the countryside and woods around Honey Creek, too. And as it happened, she knew of a house, only slightly damaged, that was probably available to buy.

"You've given me a thought, May. Thanks."

"Very nice meeting you," Lily said after she threw her daughter a quick look. "But we'd better go inside now." Then she stopped for one more thought. "When you get settled, can I twist your arm into considering volunteer work with the library? I'm trying to talk May into helping out with the children's section after school and we could use all the volunteer help we can find."

"That's a terrific idea. I would love to volunteer.

Especially with the children. I'll stop in the first chance I get."

May gave Mary a quick hug before they split up. Then Mary headed down the stairs toward her car alone. What a darling girl May Masterson was, so warm and full of smiles.

The girl seemed to be aged about fourteen. The same age Mary had been when her father had supposedly died. The stark differences between May and the child Mary had been at that age were stunning.

But when Mary thought it over, the contrast between who she was now and who she had been not too long ago was every bit as amazing. Walking toward her car, Mary considered how her life could have come so far so fast.

Yes, she alone had first decided to make changes in her life. No one had talked her into it. She remembered feeling as if the years were passing her by and that she was sick of feeling depressed all the time.

She'd found the therapist, who'd definitely helped her. And she'd lost over a hundred pounds by sheer willpower—and lots of exercise. But those didn't seem like such huge accomplishments anymore.

As she reached her car and grabbed for the door handle, Mary experienced a sudden gut feeling that someone was watching. The sun was hot this afternoon, but shivers ran down her arms.

Was this Wes's doing again? She looked around, but saw no one. Wes's office would have to be her next stop. Being followed was too creepy. She had enough problems without worrying for her safety in her own hometown. Wes needed to know that he'd gone too far.

The same way Jake had taken his act too far. *Jake*.

Yes, it was true. The biggest changes in her had come from falling in love. Jake had made her face her old fears in a way that no one else had. Too bad their relationship had been doomed from the start. It had all been a fraud. The same as most of her life had been up to now.

Were the newest changes she'd decided to make to her life also likely to be false? She didn't think so. She felt stronger than she ever had, except for all these tears. And there hadn't been any flashbacks or dreams of her childhood terrors in weeks.

As Mary sank down in the driver's seat, she tried to shake off her current depression, wishing for the pain in her heart to stop. This heavy aching in her chest was plain crazy. Even though she'd changed for the better because of loving Jake, a lasting love was not meant for someone like her. Her childhood had left her far too damaged to be loved and wanted for herself. Not for real.

In the end, she was still who she had always been. The little girl who wasn't good enough banished to the closet.

Mary found Wes in the sheriff's front office, talking to a dispatcher and a deputy. She waited for him to break free.

"Do you still have men following me around?" she demanded when the others went back to their desks.

Wes studied her carefully. "Someone has been keeping an eye on you off and on. Why do you ask?"

"I don't need protection anymore. It's feels creepy, Wes. Cut it out."

"As a matter of fact, I tend to agree with you. I don't think you need anyone following you around, either."

"Then you'll stop?"

Wes set aside the clipboard he'd been holding. "Tell me what's going on in your life. Are you back at home for good? Going back to work? I heard a rumor that you were quitting."

"Not that it's any of your business, but…"

He put his big hand on her shoulder. "I care about you, Mary. I'm asking because we're old friends and I want what's best for you."

Mary heaved a heavy sigh. She wasn't mad at Wes for wanting to protect her. He was a good man. A man of honor—not unlike Jake—except when Jake was lying. Shaking her head as the tears filled her eyes again, Mary willed away any thoughts of the man she loved. That relationship was over and done. Still, none of her pain was Wes's fault, and she could use all the friends she could get.

"I did quit my job," she told him quietly. "I'm not sure what I want to do next. Something more exciting than the library, though."

"The excitement of the past month wasn't enough for you?"

"Well, maybe not quite that exciting." She relaxed enough to chuckle at Wes's good humor and he smiled at her in return. "I'm thinking of starting my own business. I want the challenge, but I'm not sure what kind of business yet."

Wes nodded thoughtfully. "I'll keep that in mind. Maybe something will come to me." He rubbed at his chin. "Still living at home? Back on the Walsh farm?"

"Temporarily. But I'm looking to move out on my own. Maybe you could keep that in mind, too."

"I will. Every now and then I hear about a house for sale or someone looking for a roommate."

It was Mary's turn to nod thoughtfully. Wes had never given an answer about stopping her surveillance. And now he looked as though he had something more he wanted to say.

She waited for it.

"You ever give any thought to Jake these days?"

Oh, God. Not that. Could she talk about Jake without breaking down?

For Wes's sake, for the sake of keeping him as a friend, she decided to try. "Yeah. I do. A lot, actually. But…but…I'm trying to get over it."

"Why? Don't you care what he's doing? I thought you two had something going on there for a while."

She nearly choked on the sudden pain, but swallowed past the hurt. "Um, Wes, I hate to be rude. But this one is really none of your business."

"So you do still care?"

The tears welled up again and she was forced to look somewhere else for a second to push them away. "Please. Why are you doing this?"

Wes's eyebrows rose. "I thought you might want to know that Jake has left the FBI. Last time I talked to him he was in pretty sad shape. Having trouble getting over you, is my guess."

Jake quit undercover work? "I…I can't hear about him right now. I don't care—not that much."

"Hmm? And why not? Because he's basically a bad person? You and I both know he is far from that. Or maybe because he lied as part of his job? And I suppose you have never told a single lie in your entire life."

A lone tear trickled out of the corner of her eye and she brushed it away. If Wes had asked her that a few days ago, she might've had a different answer. Telling Jake she didn't love him had been her first big lie.

No. All of a sudden she realized even that wasn't the whole truth. Mary was lying to herself right now, in fact. She'd been hedging around the truth for most of her life. Her mother and brothers and Craig had never known the whole truth of how Mark Walsh had treated her and Lucy. If nothing else, that had been a lie by omission. And earlier today, she'd outright told her mother a huge untruth in order to protect Jake.

But sometimes there were good reasons for lying.

What? Did she really believe that?

"I have to g-go," she stammered. "Wes, please stop following me. I can't take it anymore."

Mary turned, walking as fast as she could without running toward the front door. All the other people in the office surreptitiously followed her with their eyes.

As she put her hand on the door handle, Wes said something very odd. "I'll try, Mary. But I can't promise anything."

"I just heard an interesting rumor, boss." Truman had finally returned to Honey Creek from his forced exile after the beating he'd taken in Bozeman a month ago. He'd been trying to get back in the boss's good graces ever since.

"I hope it's good news. I could use some about now."

"I think you'll like this one." Truman could only

hope. "You remember that fellow you were having me follow before I went on...uh...vacation? Well, my buddy in the sheriff's office told me the dude was actually an FBI agent, but that he'd quit and isn't working in law enforcement at all now. You don't still have someone tailing him, do you?"

A soft curse whooshed from the boss's lips. "That fed's already cost me plenty. No, I don't have anyone following him around anymore. Why toss good money after bad? You sure you heard this rumor right?"

Proud of himself for bringing a smile to his boss's face, Truman stood up a little taller. "Absolutely. But I can confirm it for you if you want."

"No, drop it. There's a plenty of other things you could be doing that would be more cost-effective."

"Sure. Okay. How about the Walsh girl? The one that used to be a fatty? You done with her, too?"

"Mary was never important. The only reason she was included before was that she could've identified the stalker I hired. Now that's no longer a problem and she's off the radar."

"Right." Truman bid his boss goodbye and backed out of the office feeling on top of the world.

His life was finally in order in Honey Creek. And he couldn't wait to get back to his regular job. As long as nobody ever found out what his boss had been doing in secret all these years, everything would be golden.

Chapter 16

Mary clamped her lips down on a soda cracker and used both hands to turn the steering wheel. She drove her car down the long driveway leading to the house in the woods that Jake had rented. The house where they'd been so happy. For a short time.

She'd tried to put in an offer to buy the place several times in the past couple of days. But this morning she'd finally reached a real estate agent who told her the house had already been sold.

Mary's stomach rolled. Again. But being nauseous had nothing to do with the house. She chewed on the cracker, swallowed and prayed that it would stay down.

Must be a flu bug. Perfect. Just what she needed. It was bad enough that she couldn't seem to stem the tears. Rivers of the salty liquid welled up at the worst possible moments. Her emotions had been on a real roller-coaster ride ever since she'd come back to Honey Creek. She couldn't sleep and didn't feel like eating.

Jake's image appeared everywhere she went.

Yes, she was still heartbroken over him. Maybe she always would be. After her discussion about Jake with Wes, Mary had taken the time to review everything they'd been through. Jake had used her for his assignment, true. But he'd also had real feelings for her. Mary's experience with men was extremely limited. Actually, her experience with any relationships seemed almost nonexistent. But everything inside her told her Jake had cared for her. Just not enough to make it last.

Sighing, she wished she could talk to him one more time. Tell him she wasn't mad anymore. That she understood what he'd had to do for his job. Mary had tried reaching him through the FBI, but they refused to give her his forwarding address or number. She'd only wanted to talk to him—not stalk him. But upon second—or maybe third—thought, she'd come to the conclusion that seeing him wouldn't have been smart anyway.

What could she say? That she'd been wrong? Yes, she would do so gladly. That she loved him? Well, it was true. But she wouldn't be able to bear it if he sent her away after she'd laid her heart open. And he would've. Sent her away. She wasn't the kind of woman that men yearned over forever.

Their relationship had been fast and furious. And though Jake meant the world to her, she had done something unforgivable. Called him a liar when he'd only been doing his job. She'd said terrible things, and she didn't deserve his forgiveness or his friendship.

That was part of the reason why buying this house in the woods had become important to her. It reminded her of him. Of how happy they had been during their time here.

Earlier today the agent told her that the new owner was working on remodeling the house. Mary supposed whoever it was wanted to fix up the scorched family room. She hoped they were making the place as wonderful and cozy as it had once been—and that they then would consider selling it to her for a profit.

As she pulled up in front of the house, Mary saw a small group of workmen standing around smoking cigarettes and drinking hot drinks from thermos caps. Several cars and trucks were parked along the driveway. After she slipped her sedan in behind the others and stepped out, she noticed one of the cars belonged to Wes. His sheriff's cruiser.

What was Wes doing here?

She found the sheriff standing near the cluster of other men, with his hands on his hips and his eyes trained on the part of the house under construction. When she came closer, she could hear the most god-awful-sounding racket coming from inside.

She came up beside Wes and raised her voice. "What's going on?"

He turned and his eyes widened. "Hey, I've been trying to reach you. But your cell kept going straight to voice mail."

Mary pulled the cell out of her purse. "No bars." She had to yell to be heard over the noise. "Why did you want to talk to me?"

Wes waved a hand toward the house. "That."

"What is *that?*" She turned to look at the workmen. "What're they doing?"

"They're hoping to go back to work. The commotion you hear is Jake. He says he's dismantling the house. That he wants to take it to the ground."

"Jake? My Ja— I mean, Jake Pierson?" Mary almost shook her head to clear it, ready to believe she was having a nightmare. "I don't understand. What does the new owner have to say about all of this?"

"Jake *is* the new owner. If he wants to tear the place down, I guess there's no law against it."

Now she was sure this was a dream. "Wes, please start from the beginning. What in the world is going on?"

Wes took her arm and pulled her a few feet down the driveway where they could talk in lower tones. "Jake bought the house right after he retired from the FBI. He's been fixing it up. Even hired a remodeling company to do the heavy work." Wes gestured toward the workmen.

"Meanwhile, I've been trying to talk him into starting up a new personal security and alarm business right here in Honey Creek. Thought I was making some headway with him, too, until this morning."

Crazy talk. Jake had been here in Honey Creek all along? "What happened this morning?"

Wes looked down at her with sympathetic eyes. "I drove out today to give it one more try. I told him it was time for him to stop trailing you around and start doing something productive. I even made that mandatory."

"Jake? Jake is the one who's been following me? Why?"

"I'm no psychologist, Mary. But my gut says he's

obsessing over your safety. Not entirely sure what's behind that, though."

Oh, Jake.

"When I told him he had to stop, he kind of fell apart. Ordered me and the workmen to get off his property." Wes screwed up his mouth in a scowl. "You need to talk to him. He won't listen to anyone else. That's why I've been trying to reach you. If this gets much worse, I may have to temporarily commit him to the psych ward at the Bozeman hospital. He's becoming a danger, both to others and to himself."

Mary didn't hesitate, or take the time to discuss it further. She started running toward the front door.

By the time she reached the porch steps, uncertainty about whether she'd be able to get inside slowed her down. To her astonishment, the door opened easily. She closed and locked it behind her with a quiet snick.

Turning toward the room under construction, she faced a man she barely recognized. Dear Lord, he must be having a breakdown of some sort. Jake had a chainsaw in one hand and a sledge hammer in the other, and he was ripping up newly put up drywall with a vengeance.

Construction debris, sawdust and scraps of wood flew everywhere. She blinked a couple of times and realized Jake had already demolished the back wall. Now he was moving over to attack a new stone fireplace as tears ran down his face. Tears. On the strongest male she had ever known.

Stunned, she just stared at him. He looked twenty years older than the last time she'd seen him. His shoulders slumped. His eyes were crazed with emotions she couldn't name.

Suddenly she didn't know what to do. What to say to get through to him.

But she had to get through. He couldn't keep carrying on like this. It would kill him.

While he hammered at the stone like a wild man, she calmly walked up behind him, crooning his name. Not in the least afraid, she wrapped her arms around his waist and leaned her cheek against his sweat-soaked back.

"Easy does it, Jake. Talk to me."

Stiffening in her arms, his heart pounded out a violent beat under her cheek. She could feel his whole body trembling.

But he didn't pull away. He dropped the sledge hammer and seemed to collapse in upon himself. It was as if she'd popped a balloon and all the air was slowly leaking out until nothing was left. She hung on as they eased to their knees on the floor.

"Leave me alone." His voice was tight, as though at any moment he would inflate again and explode all over the room.

"This isn't like you, Jake. Please tell me…"

He jerked out of her embrace. "You don't know what I'm like. Nobody does. I'm the liar, remember?"

Mary flinched. He couldn't have hurt her any worse if he'd slapped her in the face.

"Jake, tell me what…"

"You want to know all of it?" He laughed, and the sound sent a chill down her neck. "Fine. Why not? You already hate me. It shouldn't make much difference one way or the other if you find out I killed my wife."

Mary put her fist to her mouth to keep from making any sound that would show her surprise. But she *was* surprised. Having trouble with words, she didn't know what to say to him.

"Speechless? You should be. You—everybody—thought I was some noble man of the law. Undercover in order to fight crime. Bull! It was merely the best place for a monster to hide."

Her mumbled words spilled from her lips in double time. "You're no monster, Jake. I don't care what…"

He reached over and took her by the shoulders. "Listen to me. Listen to me tell the truth—for once in my worthless life.

"My wife was a saint." He was shaking with unspent furor. "She took me in and made me a man when nobody else would give the child of a demented survivalist the time of day. And how did I repay her?"

Jake's eyes grew crazed. Manic.

Mary wasn't frightened *of* him but *for* him. She didn't know what to say. How to calm him down. All she could do was hang on and listen.

"Tina told me we were going to have a baby. Great, right? That very night, selfish bastard that I was, I stopped thinking and became completely full of myself. Big man, I gave her my brand-new Porsche. She was thrilled and looked happier than I'd ever seen her. Said she wanted to drive it everywhere."

Mary had to break in before he exploded in grief. "She died in a car accident, Jake. It happens. That wasn't your fault." Mary worked to keep her own tears from spilling out. They weren't what Jake needed right now.

He laughed, nearing hysteria. Dug his fingers into her shoulders.

"Accident, my ass. I was a chock-full-of-myself FBI

agent who had just put one really bad dude in prison. A bastard that I'd been after for a long time. He swore to get even with me. Swore that I would pay with my life."

Jake suddenly released her and choked out a curse. "Well, I paid all right. But not with my life. My wife and unborn child took the punishment for me—dying in my car when the hit came down."

"Oh, Jake. No..." She cowered away from him, her heart torn by grief and sympathy.

"Yes," he hissed. "And what does yours truly do the very next time he falls in love? Once again, without thinking it through, I selfishly put the life of the woman I love on the line. I led the snake right to your door, Mary, and I wasn't even man enough to make you stay away from me where you would be safe."

Mary tried to speak but couldn't. Her lungs refused to breathe.

What could she do about him? With him? She was positive he wouldn't let her help him. He was so determined to be the bad guy in all of this that he would never listen to her or anyone. Shaking, she got to her feet. Crouching in a corner was the coward's way out.

She reached out her hand to help him up, still hoping to make him hear. He swatted her away and came up by himself, hands clenched, tears flowing freely down his cheeks. He was glaring at her, and his breath came in short bursts.

He was going to turn away from her. She could see it clearly in the way he stood. He wasn't going to get over this and let her in. His love for her had obviously died somewhere inside all his pain. Holding a tight rein on the sobs threatening to spill out, she almost laughed.

Of course his love had died. She wasn't the kind of woman who could keep a man. She'd never even been the sort who got what she wanted in the end. Happily-ever-afters were not meant for somebody like her.

It was all she could do not to pull him into her arms and beg. He needed help. And she wanted badly to be the one he needed. But she knew he wouldn't let her. Not now. Their time together was already over.

"Why are you here?" he finally asked.

"Wes asked me to talk to you. He's worried about you. I'm worried, too."

"Both of you need to leave me the hell alone. I'm not worth your time."

"You need to talk to a therapist, Jake." If he wouldn't let her be the one, then he had to find a professional. "Let *someone* help you."

He was trying to focus his eyes on her face. "Why aren't you running the other way?"

Because she loved him.

"You don't strike me as a masochist, Mary." He waved his arm as if shooing her away. "Stay close to me and sooner or later you'll pay with your life."

"You planning on hurting me?"

He narrowed his eyes and scowled. "No."

"You planning on hurting yourself?"

It was then that he looked around and saw the destruction that he'd wrought. "No."

Mary was exhausted. She could barely see straight. But Jake needed her to make good sense. Maybe not forever, but for now.

"You're tired, Jake. Go upstairs and lie down. Things will look better after you've rested."

"Walk away."

She heard the fear in his voice. He didn't want to be alone. She couldn't say that she blamed him.

Reaching out with compassion, she took him by the hand and together they climbed the stairs the way they had done many times in the past. Only this time, when they lay down on the bed, they were fully clothed.

Within minutes Jake fell into a deep, profound sleep. And Mary cradled him in her arms while he did.

Later, she slipped out of the bed and dragged herself down the stairs. She didn't want to be here when he woke up. Not if he wouldn't let her help him. Love him.

She had to get on with her life. Wes would help him. Maybe better than she could.

So tired she wasn't sure she could make it out to her car, all Mary wanted was to curl up in bed until she was over the flu. Then she would find a place to live that wouldn't remind her of Jake.

He needed professional help. Mary only hoped that he would get it soon. But she would probably never know whether he had or not.

Silent tears formed again in her eyes, and she frantically shoved them aside. Mary needed to keep all that hurt locked up inside so no one else ever guessed. But she'd done that kind of thing before.

Mary reminded herself that for once in her life, she had been lucky enough to fall in love with someone who had loved her back. Maybe their relationship had only been temporary. But many women never even got that lucky. She'd been blessed by having this experience.

And she would always have her memories.

Jake thanked Mary's sister Lucy and then headed up the stairs from her shop to the apartment above. It had

taken him days to steel himself, but he was on his way
to talk to Mary at last. She'd moved off the farm and
was living here at her sister's place.

They needed to talk. How could he have let her walk
away without at least thanking her for listening to his
confession? She'd been right. Despite his misgivings, it
had been important for him to talk to a therapist. He'd
finally seen one. And he would continue. He needed to
thank her for that, too.

Mary Walsh had been right about everything from
the start. She was a lifesaver and had given him much
more than he could've imagined: compassion, love,
tenderness. And, damn him, he'd been so totally
absorbed with his own pain that he had let her walk
away without a word.

It fascinated him how different Mary's personality
was from Tina's. Mary was much stronger and smarter
about a lot of things. But she didn't have the self-
assurance and knowledge of her own worth that his
wife had possessed. Life had conspired against Mary.
She'd never felt safe enough or certain enough of her
abilities to explore.

But Jake felt absolutely certain. She was worth the
world to him. He missed her so badly that he could
barely breathe until he had her back in his arms again.

Saying a silent prayer that she would be willing to
take a chance on a man only half done finding out what
mattered the most, he straightened his shoulders and
approached her door.

Breathing in, Jake held his breath and knocked. When
Mary answered, she looked stunningly beautiful. And
all the air blew right back out of him.

Her skin glowed as she looked up at him. "Jake?"

Like the fool he was, he choked on his own anxiety before he could speak. "Can we talk?"

"Come in." She looked confused. Scared.

Jake didn't like seeing either expression in her eyes. He wanted to see only love when she looked at him. She'd had love in her eyes once. Now it was up to him to put it back.

But he needed to deserve her love.

"How have you been?" He studied her face for a clue as to how she was feeling about him.

"I've missed you." They both said the words at the same time and then smiled tentatively.

Still standing just inside the closed door, they looked at each other. Jake's fingers ached to touch her, but he fisted his hands at his sides instead.

"What brought you here, Jake?" Was that hope that he heard in her voice?

His own hope bubbled up, threatening to spill all over the room. "I came to…uh…say a couple of things."

Her eyes narrowed, and she looked more uncertain than ever. "Why are you really here? Have you heard something about me being sick?"

His turn to be confused. "I haven't heard anything. You don't look sick. Are you?"

She shook her head, turned and waved her hand to convey that she wanted him to continue with his explanation.

"I came to apologize for being such an ass and for spilling my guts to you the way I did." He tried softening his tone. "I came to thank you for listening and to tell you I've been seeing a psychologist."

She blinked up at him. "Sometimes burdens seem

better when they're shared by two people. I'm only glad I could help."

He couldn't stand it. She looked so unsure of herself.

Reaching out, he stroked her cheek, still wishing he could take her in his arms. "You're right again. You have a bad habit of doing that, you know. I'm here asking if you'd be willing to share a couple of more burdens with me."

"What kind of burdens?"

"Well, for one thing, I own a huge house that badly needs redecorating. I've come to the conclusion that it needs a woman's special touch. Your touch.

"And for another thing," he added quickly. "I'm starting up a business and have discovered I'm terrible at administration—all those details. I thought you might consider becoming my partner."

"Oh." The hope grew brighter in her eyes. "Why?"

"Because I love you. And I thought that you…"

"I love you, too." She jumped into his arms and snuggled into his embrace.

Thank God.

He held her close and whispered, "I can't live without you. If you can accept that deep down I'm a selfish bastard, but one who is trying to change, give us a chance. Love me. Marry me. Teach me how to give."

She looked up at him. Her eyes were bright and full of love. It would be too easy to lose himself there.

"I have a burden of my own to share first," she said with a whimsical, lopsided smile. "After I tell you, ask me again."

He held his breath once more and waited.

"I'm pregnant. You and I are going to be parents."

"What?" Jake was having trouble processing the words. This couldn't be happening. Not again. Pure panic spiked his pulse.

"Jake?" Mary pulled out of his arms and put her hands on her hips. "Listen to me. I'm not going to die. Our baby won't die. It isn't happening again. I'm healthy and the baby is healthy. And under no circumstances will I accept any kind of gifts from you. I promise. We'll live long and happy lives. Now, will you marry me?"

Trying to smile, he opened his mouth to form the word but it wouldn't come. Tears built up behind his eyes as he nodded and reached for her.

The tears were a surprise. He'd thought he was all done with them. But the crazy happiness felt familiar.

The most wonderful woman in the whole world would be teaching him how to give. And he would give her anything in return. Tears included. Anything that made her happy.

Then he did something not surprising at all. He kissed her. A simple, I-do kind of kiss. Reminding her of who loved her. Of who was willing to share her burdens from now on.

They would live long and happy lives. Giving and loving and sharing. Together. Forever.

Epilogue

"How thrilling, honey. When do you two plan on being married? I hope we'll have enough time to throw a huge bash." Jolene took a sip of wine and relaxed back next to Craig on Mary and Jake's brand-new sofa.

Mary was so pleased with herself that all she wanted to do was laugh. This was their first real dinner party. Well, it couldn't be called a real party. But it was the first time they'd invited family over. Everything felt just perfect. How good could one life be?

"Yes, Mom, we'll have enough time. I've always wanted a winter wedding. After the holidays. January maybe."

Jake cleared his throat and squeezed her arm lightly. "Can you give me a hand in the kitchen?"

She nodded and stood. "Excuse us. Craig, do you need another drink?"

When Craig looked her way and shook his head, she noticed the corners of his eyes were crinkled and tight. As though he were in pain.

Jake didn't give her time to think; he hustled them both into the kitchen. Once there, he drew her into his arms and kissed her. Another of his fantastic toe-curling kisses that pledged more to come later.

After they split apart to draw in air, she laughed at his urgent desperation, but she felt it, too. "Jolene and Craig won't be here much longer. We're already on the after-dinner drinks. Save some of those kisses for when we're alone, please."

"There's lots more where that came from, woman." Jake looked down at her in his arms as though he was ready to have her for dessert. She knew exactly how he felt.

When she turned to get the coffee, he pulled her back against his chest. "How are you feeling? You look spectacular tonight."

"Thank you, kind sir. I'm feeling well. Being sick to my stomach only seems to come in the mornings now. And I've been extra good tonight, too. No alcohol, of course. And not a lot of empty calories. You should be proud of me."

Jake rubbed his hand along her spine and the temperature soared between them. "Oh, I am. Except for the part where you haven't told your mother and Craig about the baby yet. Shouldn't they know?"

Mary sighed. "I wanted to leave it between us for a little longer. I'll tell them soon."

She wasn't used to sharing. Or being the center of attention. But she was working up to it. She hoped she wouldn't show for a few more months, and she was savoring every precious moment of building a relationship with Jake before the baby came into the picture.

A child would change their relationship once again. And though she couldn't wait to be a mother, she wanted to hold on for a while to the feeling of being loved as a woman and a wife first.

"Did you notice Craig looks like he's in pain?" Mary turned to face the coffeemaker and talked to Jake over her shoulder.

She could hear the shrug in his voice. "Not sure."

Mary grimaced. "Well, for Mom's sake I hope it isn't anything real bad, like his heart. The two of them are only just now admitting how much they love each other. It's their turn to be happy."

Jake put his arms around Mary's waist and kissed the back of the neck. "It's our turn, too, sweetheart. I never thought I could be this lucky—to get a second chance at love."

He snuggled her close and she reveled in the wondrous experience of having someone care. "And I do love you, Mary. I won't ever stop telling you. You are my heart and my life. My nights and my mornings. Give me your burdens and take mine for as long as we both live."

Mary leaned her head back on his shoulder and smiled to herself, loving the feel of his body against hers. And loving the heartfelt words of the very special man who loved her that much.

It occurred to her then that she had never read any words more wonderful, not in any book. Jake's love was better than a bestseller.

* * * * *

COMING NEXT MONTH

Available August 31, 2010

#1623 CAVANAUGH REUNION
Cavanaugh Justice
Marie Ferrarella

#1624 THE LIBRARIAN'S SECRET SCANDAL
The Coltons of Montana
Jennifer Morey

#1625 PROTECTOR'S TEMPTATION
Marilyn Pappano

#1626 MESMERIZING STRANGER
New Man in Town
Jennifer Greene

ROMANTIC SUSPENSE

SRSCNM0810

REQUEST YOUR FREE BOOKS!

2 FREE NOVELS PLUS 2 FREE GIFTS!

ROMANTIC SUSPENSE

Sparked by Danger, Fueled by Passion.

Enjoy a sneak peek at fan favorite Molly O'Keefe's
Harlequin Superromance miniseries,
THE NOTORIOUS O'NEILLS, *with*
TYLER O'NEILL'S REDEMPTION,
available September 2010
only from Harlequin Superromance.

Police chief Juliette Tremblant recognized the shape of the man strolling down the street—in as calm and leisurely fashion as if it were the middle of the day rather than midnight. She slowed her car, convinced her eyes were playing tricks on her. It had been a long time since Tyler O'Neill had been seen in this town.

As she pulled to a stop at the curb, he turned toward her, and her heart about stopped.

"What the hell are you doing here, Tyler?"

"Well, if it isn't Juliette Tremblant." He made his way over to her, then leaned down so he could look her in the eye. He was close enough to touch.

Juliette was not, repeat, *not* going to touch Tyler O'Neill. Not with her fingers. Not with a ten-foot pole. There would be no touching. Which was too bad, since it was the only way she was ever going to convince herself the man standing in front of her—as rumpled and heart-stoppingly handsome now as he'd been at sixteen—was real.

And not a figment of all her furious revenge dreams.

"What are you doing back in Bonne Terre?" she asked.

"The manor is sitting empty," Tyler said and shrugged, as though his arriving out of the blue after ten years was casual. "Seems like someone should be watching over the family home."

"You?" She laughed at the very notion of him being here for any unselfish reason. "Please."

He stared at her for a second, then smiled. Her heart fluttered against her chest—a small mechanical bird powered by that smile.

"You're right." But that cryptic comment was all he offered.

Juliette bit her lip against the other questions.

Why did you go?

Why didn't you write? Call?

What did I do?

But what would be the point? Ten years of silence were all the answer she really needed.

She had sworn off feeling anything for this man long ago. Yet one look at him and all the old hurt and rage resurfaced as though they'd been waiting for the chance. That made her mad.

She put the car in gear, determined not to waste another minute thinking about Tyler O'Neill. "Have a good night, Tyler," she said, liking all the cool "go screw yourself" she managed to fit into those words.

It seems Juliette has an old score to settle with Tyler.
Pick up TYLER O'NEILL'S REDEMPTION
to see how he makes it up to her.
Available September 2010,
only from Harlequin Superromance.

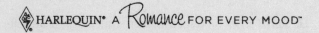